THE ACCIDENTALS

Guadalupe Nettel is a Mexican author of award-winning novels and short story collections. Her work has been translated into more than twenty languages and adapted for theatre and film. *Still Born*, her most recent novel, was shortlisted for the 2023 International Booker Prize. In 2008 she received a PhD in Literature from the EHESS in Paris. She has edited cultural and literary magazines such as *Número Cero* and *Revista de la Universidad de México*. She lives in Paris as a writer in residence at the Columbia University Institute for Ideas and Imagination.

Rosalind Harvey is a literary translator and educator. She has translated writers such as Juan Pablo Villalobos, Katya Adaui and Elvira Navarro, and her work has been shortlisted for the Guardian First Book Award and the Oxford-Weidenfeld Translation Prize, among others. She is a Fellow of the Royal Society of Literature, an Arts Foundation Fellow and a founding member of the Emerging Translators Network, and currently teaches on the MA in Literary Translation at the University of Warwick.

'Guadalupe Nettel yet again walks into uncertain terrain with these mysterious stories. There are secrets everywhere, she says, especially in life's most intimate and familiar aspects. *The Accidentals* never loses its sense of things being out of joint, and Nettel explores these fears with calm and with beauty.'
— Mariana Enríquez, author of *Our Share of Night*

'I adored this collection, it spread its roots out within me. Nettel is an extraordinary writer.'
— Daisy Johnson, author of *The Hotel*

'*The Accidentals* is a striking and compelling collection that searches for the extraordinary within the ordinary. Each narrative veers seamlessly from the mundane to the existential; the writing is deft and unsettling prose imbues the work with a profound resonance. I loved these stories, mad and controlled, and brilliant.'
— Elaine Feeney, author of *All the Good Things You Deserve*

'Nettel is one of the leading lights in contemporary Latin American literature.... I envy how naturally she makes use of language; her resistance to ornamentation and artifice; and the almost stoic fortitude with which she dispenses her profound and penetrating knowledge of human nature.'
— Valeria Luiselli, author of *Lost Children Archive*

'I love the work of Guadalupe Nettel, one of Mexico's greatest living writers. Her fiction is brilliant and original, always suffused with sensuality and strange science.'
— Paul Theroux, author of *The Mosquito Coast*

'Nettel is free. She has succeeded in creating an audacious narrative style all her own, a singular and fearless way of being in the world. An essential voice of the new Latin American literature.'
— Enrique Vila-Matas, author of *Mac's Problem*

'The stories in *The Accidentals* move through a landscape that is both foreign and familiar, mysterious and menacing, dreamy and distraught, and I had the palpable sense that anything might happen next. It is the kind of book you read in a single afternoon, gladly relinquishing the cares of day-to-day life to sink into its otherworldly submersions.'
— Jessie Ren Marshall, author of *Women! In! Peril!*

Praise for *Still Born*

'In *Still Born*, Guadalupe Nettel renders with great veracity life as it is encountered in the everyday, taking us to the heart of the only things that really matter: life, death and our relationships with others. All of these are contained in the experience of motherhood, which this novel explores and deepens.'
— Annie Ernaux, author of *The Years*

'Deeply intelligent, *Still Born* is a propulsive novel with a depth of feeling so woven into the language that it never feels worn or applied. The denatured quality of the tone means the ideas of the book – the suspicion of the body as having incompatible desires from the mind; the impulses versus the aversions to child-having; the complexities of the mother-child dynamic – all just absolutely sing. I loved it.'
— Susannah Dickey, author of *Common Decency*

'This highly original novel, in an excellent translation by Rosalind Harvey, pursues a range of ideas connected to children, who should have them and who should take care of them.... There's a dark undertow to *Still Born* that reminded me of Elena Ferrante's novels.'
— Miranda France, *TLS*

'*Still Born* is an astonishingly elegant, intelligent, affecting novel, which has stayed in my mind from the moment I began it to long after I finished. I felt a huge sense of relief that I had encountered a work of art about ambivalence in mothering, which encompassed a true, authentic range of emotions and curiosities – vanity, aggression, jealousy and selfishness – with sanguine acceptance, as well as the beautiful and difficult project of giving and sustaining love which marks all our lives, mothers or otherwise.'
—— Megan Nolan, author of *Acts of Desperation*

'*Still Born* is a startling novel about whatever it is that drives adults to take care of children, and all the many things that make that care painful and sometimes impossible. There is a quiet force to the poised and deliberate writing. The novel is a deep exploration of affection and vulnerability.'
—— Caleb Klaces, author of *Fatherhood*

'*Still Born* is a rare thing: an unsentimental analysis of the ambivalences and moral complexity of motherhood. It is a book which demands to be discussed, at length, with friends, and I longed to do so.'
—— Jessie Greengrass, author of *The High House*

'I read *Still Born* in less than a day. It is perfect: deeply feminist, wise, funny and alive. Nettel is generous to each of her characters, and in prose that is crisp and light. I love this book.'
—— Yara Rodrigues Fowler, author of *there are more things*

'Rosalind Harvey skilfully translates the original Spanish into precise and plain, but deeply moving, prose. Without resorting to sentimentality, the novel charts its characters' halting efforts to understand and comfort one another. It is a piercing reflection on the ways acts of care bind people together.'
—— *Economist*

Fitzcarraldo Editions

THE ACCIDENTALS

GUADALUPE NETTEL

Translated by
ROSALIND HARVEY

CONTENTS

IMPRINTING [15]

THE FELLOWSHIP OF ORPHANS [27]

PLAYING WITH FIRE [35]

THE PINK DOOR [53]

A FOREST UNDER THE EARTH [71]

LIFE ELSEWHERE [83]

THE ACCIDENTALS [97]

THE TORPOR [111]

For Mir, Lorenzo and Mateo

'We don't see things as they are, we see them as we are.'
— Anaïs Nin

IMPRINTING

Before he died, my uncle was in hospital for three weeks. I found out due to a coincidence, or what the surrealists used to call 'objective chance', to describe those fortuitous events that seem dictated by our destiny. Around this time, my best friend Verónica's mother was suffering from very late-stage cancer and was a patient in the intensive care unit at the same clinic. One morning, Verónica had asked me to go with her to visit her mother, and I couldn't say no. We left the university, which was in the same neighbourhood, and, instead of going to our Latin etymology class, we got on the bus. As I wandered through the corridors waiting for Verónica to attend to her mother, I amused myself by reading the names of patients on the doors. Seeing my uncle's was enough to understand he was a relative, but it took me some time to figure out who he was. After several seconds of confusion – a feeling comparable to when we discover in a cemetery a tombstone with our surname on it, with no idea to whom it belongs – I realized that the sick man was Frank, my mother's older brother. I was aware of his existence, but I didn't know him. He was the exiled relative of my family, as it were, a man nobody mentioned out loud, let alone in front of my mum. Despite being filled with curiosity at that moment, I didn't dare stick my head into the room lest he recognize me. An absurd fear, really, since as far as I knew we'd never met.

I stayed there for a good while, not knowing what to do, concentrating on my heartbeat, which only grew faster and faster, until the door opened and two women dressed in white emerged from the room. One of them was holding a breakfast tray with dirty plates on it.

'That man eats more than a St. Bernard. Who would have thought it in his state?'

It amused me to find out that the nurses joked about their patients, as did the possibility that my uncle was an imaginary invalid like Molière's, whom we were reading in my drama class.

On the bus on the way back to the university, I told Verónica about my discovery. I also told her everything I knew about Frank. A good student from primary school up until the final year of exams, he had obtained an impeccable reputation at school, as well as the admiration of all his teachers. He was always able to count on my grandmother's collusion for this – as I once heard my mother say – because she would provide excuses for his absences from class, as well as his antics at home. After completing one year of an engineering degree, he quit to devote himself to photography, and then later on to wandering the globe. My relatives spoke too about his vices and addictions, but I never heard anyone specify exactly what sort these were. He was never present for the big events in my family, my brother's graduation or my fifteenth birthday, occasions where gaggles of relatives would sprout as if by spontaneous generation and to whom I had to introduce myself several times over. All of my uncles would be there, apart from Frank. On occasion I would hear old friends of my parents ask after him with morbid curiosity, as you might ask after someone when you know, without a shadow of a doubt, that there will be some sort of hilarious new titbit. It was impossible, at least for me, not to notice how uncomfortable my mother was when answering questions about her brother's whereabouts. *I know he's in Asia*, she would say, or, *He's still with his girlfriend, the sculptor*. The things I knew about him I had heard in passing, as in those instances, but at the time, Frank's life didn't interest me a great deal.

The following day I asked Verónica if she would let me accompany her to the hospital. This time we missed a linguistics and phonology class, the most boring of all. We got to the hospital at around midday. Once my friend had gone into her mother's room, I waited a few minutes and then, after making sure there were no nurses in Frank's room, I knocked at the door and went in. It was the first time I stood before his bed, a place I would return to many times. My uncle was a robust-looking man with a shock of grey hair who did not, in effect, have the appearance of a sick man. What he did have was a combination of features very like my own. His expression, unlike the other patients, such as Verónica's mother, was lucid, and he was conscious of everything happening around him. His left arm was connected via a catheter to a drip containing all sorts of medicines, but aside from this, and from a slight paralysis down the left-hand side of his face, he seemed ready to leap out of bed.

'We don't know each other,' I said. 'I'm Antonia, your niece.'

For a second or two I felt as if, rather than being a pleasant surprise, my presence had frightened him. It was a fleeting sensation, the brief flash caused by intuition, but as unmistakable to me as the shock I had felt the previous day when standing outside his door. Before replying, a seductive smile crossed his face, the same one he would offer me every time I went to visit him.

I've always thought it strange the familiarity we establish with someone unknown as soon as we find out they are related to us. I'm sure this has nothing to do with an immediate affinity, but rather with something artificial, such as culture, a conventional allegiance to the clan or, as some say, a surname. This, however, was not what took place between my uncle and me that morning. I don't know if it was because of the irreverent reputation he enjoyed among my relatives, or the disobedience implied by having anything to do with him; the fact is, I felt an admiration similar to that evoked by characters from legend.

He asked me how I had found him and requested that I didn't tell anyone. There was no way he wanted to get back in touch with my family. To reassure him, I explained that it had been by accident. I told him about Verónica and her mother, and assured him that he could count on my silence.

For the first few days, I found the smell of the hospital and of my uncle unbearable. And so instead of sitting in the visitors' chair next to his bed, I positioned myself on a concrete ledge by the window, which let in a pleasant breeze. I was there for over an hour, replying to the questions he asked me about university, my literary tastes, my political opinions. It was the first time someone in my family was taking seriously the fact that I was studying literature, without thinking that my choice was down to a lack of talent for anything else or that it was a degree aimed at women who hoped to devote their entire lives to marriage. It also surprised me how much he had read. There wasn't a single one of the writers I mentioned that morning of whom he hadn't read at least one book. Then Verónica gave a knock and, from the doorway, signalled for me to come out.

I didn't kiss him goodbye. I held out my hand without looking at him with a shyness he seemed to find amusing, then walked to the door.

'Come back soon,' he said.

On the bus, my friend grilled me.

'He's still so handsome,' she remarked eagerly. 'He must

have been quite a looker as a young man. Be careful though – there must be a reason your family's not keen on him.'

It was a Thursday. We were in the middle of the rainy season and I arrived home dripping wet. My mother and my brothers would be out until late, so the kitchen and all the bedrooms were dark. I put down my books and, without wasting any time, went straight to the study to look for the box where my mother kept all her childhood photographs: two carefully assembled albums that recorded her first few years of life. There she was with my uncle Amadeo and an older boy with enormous dark brown eyes, who could be none other than Frank. In several of these pictures they were smiling and playing in a swimming pool, a park, or in my grandparents' back yard. After the first few pages, the older boy mysteriously disappeared. Outside these photo albums, there were other loose photos in the bottom of the box. In these, my mum must have been in her early thirties. Her clothes were unusually bohemian: huipiles and skirts with indigenous embroidery, bell-bottoms, copious bangles. My brother and I would appear from time to time in our parents' arms, wearing pyjamas or underwear. In the most recent ones, I must have been five or six years old. Many of these photos had been systematically cropped. I suspected, and I don't think I was wrong, that the part that had been censored was actually Frank's head or entire torso. Probably, in some remote period, he had lived with us, something my mother had never mentioned. The way the paper had been cut made it easy to imagine the furious action of the scissors. What could he have done to deserve such a vicious attack? And in any case, why had the childhood photos, where they all seemed so close, not been removed as well? I thought about Juan, my own brother, three years older than me. Ever since he'd become a teenager, we inhabited the same house with no camaraderie whatsoever. The closeness we had forged during childhood had been forgotten some while ago. Nevertheless, it would never have occurred to me to remove his silhouette from family photos. I heard a key turn in the door. My brother was back from university with a couple of friends and they went to sit in the dining room. I put the box back on the shelf in the study and returned to my room without a sound.

The next morning, I went back to the hospital. No sooner had I entered than I noticed a satisfied expression on my uncle's face. This time I was the one who asked the questions. I asked him to tell me his story from when he lived in my grandparents' house, what his childhood had been like, and his experience at university. His account did not contradict the one I had heard from my family, but he added a dose of scorn and humour that made it far more enjoyable. In his version, the family dramas became comedies, and the reactions of each member of the family a faithful caricature. In almost twenty years he hadn't forgotten any of their personalities and imitated them to a tee, making me burst out laughing several times. The only one who escaped his barbs was my mother. That week I found out about a number of family secrets: my aunt Laura's first experiences of love, which led her to have an abortion; my father's compulsive jealousy; the mysterious death of a neighbour, which some attributed to my grandfather... If they all had some dark episode in their past, why had he been the only one to be cast out?

I asked him as delicately as I could, and he replied that he had been the one to cut off all contact so as not to feel judged on his acts and his choices.

'But don't you miss having the support of a family?'

'If I liked families, don't you think I would have formed my own?'

I must have opened my eyes wider than was expected because my uncle burst out laughing.

'Don't make that face! In time you'll see I'm right. You're not like the others. I could see that even when you were little.'

His comment made me shiver. I was flattered that Frank considered me cleverer than the rest of our relatives, in whom I too saw countless defects, but at the same time, it frightened me to be different. Even though I liked literature, even though I was drawn to transgressive, eccentric people like him, I did want to get married and have children. The thought of not achieving this worried me immensely, especially the idea that I might one day find myself in hospital without anyone's support.

'So you'd already met me?'

In response, Frank took my hand. It was the first time he had touched me – at least that I remember – but in his warm, protective palm I felt, despite the circumstances, an indisputable intimacy. Somewhere, probably in one of those educational magazines that were always lying around at my grandparents' house, I had read something about the traces left in our memory by the touch and scent of those we come into contact with in the first few years of our lives. *Imprinting*, I think it's called. According to the article, this bodily mark is where family ties are cemented. We remained like that for a few more minutes, his larger hand covering mine. Not even the presence of the nurses made us let go of each other. For me it was a silent pact, the tacit promise that I wasn't going to leave him there to his fate.

It was the start of the weekend. Even with the pretext of accompanying Verónica, it would be difficult for me to be out of the house without drawing attention to myself. What's more, on the Saturday we had a wedding to go to, and then a lunch on the Sunday.

When I explained this to Frank, he asked that I at least try to call him on the phone.

'I was quite peaceful here before you showed up. Now that I've found you, I suspect I'm going to miss you.' I assured him that I felt the same.

Before going back to university, I asked to speak with his doctor. The specialist wasn't around at that point, but the person on call was able to give me a few explanations: Frank had a tumour in his brain that had been there for several years and it was no longer possible to give him any treatment, aside from palliative care.

I had to go and hide in the toilet so Verónica wouldn't see me cry. She who tried with all her might to keep herself afloat while her mother lay dying – what would she have thought if she'd found me in floods of tears for someone I barely knew?

The time I spent in the company of my family but away from him seemed interminable. At the wedding, I made a great effort not to laugh, remembering his imitations of all of them. I would have preferred a thousand times over to be in his hospital room with its smell of disinfectant rather than to listen to their repetitive conversations. I thought about how different all our family get-togethers would have been if he had been present. The reasons you can fall into disgrace with your own relatives are strange, so very strange. Over the years I have observed all kinds of cases, and I've come to believe that they are hardly ever down to questions of morality or principles, but rather to internal betrayals, perhaps invisible to outsiders' eyes, but unforgivable to the clan to whom they belong, or at least, to certain members. On Sunday morning, as I helped my mother make lunch, I tried to broach the subject.

'What did Uncle Frank do for you to stop talking to

him?' I asked, trying to play down the issue. Her answer was short but unequivocal.

'He behaved like an idiot.'

She was in a good mood that day, and the levity with which she received my question reassured me. She promptly left the kitchen to go and see to her guests.

On Monday morning, when I returned to the hospital, I found Frank with a respirator over his mouth. I tried to hide how upset I was. I made some joke about the apparatus and he smiled beneath the mask.

That day we began the custom of watching films together on his laptop. First, we put on *Blow-Up*, and then *The Best Intentions*. I sat in the visitors' chair and, from there, we once again took each other's hands, touching each other quite casually. They were easy caresses, distracted, almost, on the nape of the neck or along the arms, but to me they seemed delicious. We spent hours like that, feeling the other's skin prickle, while on the screen a story took place to which we barely paid attention.

Every afternoon on the bus ride back, I would recount these visits to Verónica. I told her of the affection I felt for my uncle and gave her detailed clips of our approaches towards one another: *today he brushed against my lips, today the edge of my ear*. Until one afternoon, my friend made it clear that I could not by any means count on her complicity.

'You need to wake up,' she said, sharply. 'You're running a serious risk. To be honest, you'd be better off not coming to the hospital any more'.

It was shortly afterwards, perhaps a day or two later, when she unexpectedly opened the door to our room and announced that her mother had fallen into a coma. Verónica howled rather than sobbed, and although it was entirely justified in these circumstances, I found it intolerable that Frank should see her like this. And so I suggested we go down to the cafeteria. Once there, she ordered a coffee and let the cup grow cold between her hands. I, on the other hand, drank mine quickly, wanting to return as soon as possible to the ICU, but not daring to leave her alone. Neither of us said a word. She stared intently at her coffee, I at the visitors going back and forth through the main door of the hospital. In the middle of this mass of people, I caught sight of my grandmother, along with my mum and my uncle Amadeo.

'They're going to Frank's room!' I said to Verónica, in despair. 'How can they have found out he's here?'

'I told them,' she confessed, without looking up. 'Forgive me, but I felt someone ought to protect you.'

I nearly slapped her.

'Go home and act as if nothing's happened. Do it now while they're heading upstairs.'

Instead of following her advice, I ran out towards the lift to catch them up. As soon as the doors opened, I heard my mother's worried voice from a way off, but her words were unintelligible. Once I was outside Frank's room, I pressed my face to the door to listen. All I managed to hear was the following: ...*Twenty years, and when you find her, you try to do the same thing to her!* At this moment a nurse came past with the medicine trolley and gave me a conspiratorial smile. My uncle's answer was drowned out by the tinkling of the jars of medication. I wondered how many family secrets were revealed in this ward every week or, in contrast, would remain hidden forever. I couldn't wait any longer and opened the door without caring about the consequences. As soon as I was inside, a silence fell, interrupted only by the heart monitor, which, with its oscillating graph, revealed Frank's agitation. The air in the room was oppressive. There was hurt on my mother's face, and humiliation on my uncle's. I felt sad for them both.

Without saying another word, my mother took me by the arm like she used to when I was little. I felt the pressure of her tense fingers on my skin, the same fingers that had fed me, dressed me and embraced me my entire life. No ideology, not even the tenderness my uncle elicited in me, could resist her touch. Among all the imprinting marks of my childhood, hers was without doubt the strongest. I allowed her to lead me towards the exit and then to the car park where she had left her car. My grandmother and Amadeo stayed in the room. I wondered what it would be like for Frank to have his mother's hands near him.

I had a sleepless night, observing the different intensities of the rain. I must have got up at least ten times to see if my grandmother had come back home. On one of these excursions, it occurred to me to go to the study and look for the photographs I had seen a couple of weeks ago. This time I didn't stop to look at the album. I spread the cut-up images out on the carpet like someone about to do a jigsaw puzzle. My task was to imagine or deduce what the missing pieces were. My parents' bedroom was at the other end of the house. The risk of them surprising me was minimal. What didn't occur to me is that, just like me, my mother was also suffering from insomnia that night. When there was no longer space for a single other photo on the floor, I realized she was watching me silently from the doorway. Her long nightgown that fell to her ankles gave her the appearance of a ghost. Her swollen eyes betrayed the fact that she'd recently been crying. I stayed silent for a few minutes to see if she might feel like giving me some sort of explanation, but my strategy failed and I chose not to insist. Outside, it had stopped raining. My mum sat down next to me and helped me to gather up the photographs. When we had finished, we put the box back in its place and sat down on the sofa to wait for the sun to come up in silence. I looked at my mum out of the corner of my eye and found her lost in her own ruminations. She too must have had a lot of questions without answers which, out of respect for me, she was choosing not to put into words.

That day I went to the clinic without having set foot in any of the classrooms at the university. My grandmother was there and she greeted me with a face deformed by exhaustion. I asked her to leave us alone for a moment and, to my surprise, she accepted without a word. Frank was semi-conscious. Moving doubtfully, I put my hand under the covers and took his, searching for some kind of answer. The only thing I found on his skin that morning, however, was a piece of cold, inert flesh, a touch that was entirely unrecognizable.

THE FELLOWSHIP OF ORPHANS

I never knew my parents. I grew up in a public institution where I shared a room with fifteen other children who cried, as I did, in their bunkbeds at night whenever they thought about the families they had lost or the ones they wished they had. It was a discreet weeping, but as contagious as the flu or the chicken pox, which we also contracted during those years, and which covered our faces with scars. One child would start sobbing in their bed and that was enough for it to spread throughout the whole dormitory; it was as if a tap had been turned on and the room would be flooded with tears. During the day, the differences between us were quite evident: some sullen and short-tempered, others demure and well-behaved, some athletic, or more given to games of strategy; but at night we were all orphans, and this pain brought us together as if in fellowship, to the point where now – many decades later – we still seek each other out. Sometimes, at a wedding, a wake or some other social gathering, I will come face to face with someone else like me. They don't need to tell me their story: there is something in their gaze, in the way they move or communicate that makes it obvious, perhaps not to others, but certainly to me. On several occasions I have been able to identify members of this fellowship, the fellowship of those who used to cry at night for the same reason and who, from time to time, still do.

Unlike several of my classmates who had lived at one point with a grandparent, perhaps an aunt, or an alcoholic relative, from whose arms they were eventually wrested, I never had any information about my family. My oldest memories take place in the playground or the dining room of the orphanage, surrounded by a wild pack of wounded, unfulfilled creatures. I spent years of my childhood inventing all kinds of stories about where I had come from. In one, my parents had died in a fire or a car accident of which I was the sole survivor. Their bodies were so disfigured by flames or the impact that it had been impossible to identify them. In another, my mother was a teenager who fell accidentally pregnant and whose parents had taken the baby away from her just after it had been born. There are so many reasons that can explain the forced separation of a mother from her child... In most of these stories, my family was still alive and wanted to be reunited with me just as much as I did. Even though all the searches I have attempted – whether in the archives of my school or in the many hospitals across the city – have failed, even though I have never managed to find out either my mother's name or my real date of birth, I have to admit that I continue to believe in miracles.

It was no doubt prompted by this optimistic tendency that the other day, when I came across a 'MISSING PERSON' poster on a lamp-post in Parque Acacias, I felt it was a sign from fate. Almost all the posters that appear in the streets about missing persons are for women. They are the ones who, without a doubt, vanish most frequently, and very seldom voluntarily. Old people and children do so, too. These posters always make me exceedingly sad, and yet I always look at them. Not only do I sniff them out immediately, but I also read them in their entirety, including the phone numbers, as if this gesture of solidarity were the least I could do for all those suddenly embroiled in such an anguishing situation. The poster that day reported the disappearance of a man called Manu Carrillo. He was thirty-two years old and six feet tall. The photo accompanying it showed a man with brown hair, an oval face and large eyes. Although the text on the poster claimed he lacked any distinguishing features, it was possible to make out a certain intense and perhaps tormented expression, judging by the unusually dark bags under his eyes that spread out as far as down as the top of his cheekbones. *Last seen on 15 March at home. If you find him, please inform Mrs Gloria Carrillo immediately*, and then a phone number. I guessed straight away that this woman was the man's mother, and I imagined her pacing inconsolably around the house. I looked at the date on my watch. It was 5 April. If the poster was still current, the woman had spent almost three weeks without any news of her son. I recalled that, on occasion, a child would escape from the orphanage, taking their chance when there was a trip to the cinema or some lapse on the part of the cleaners or teachers, who would come in and out of the building throughout the day. When this happened, all of us would without exception set to searching frantically. Most of the time the child came back of their own accord, a little before nightfall. Then we would all be called into the dining room to be scolded. They would tell us how lucky we were to live there and how grateful we should be to not find ourselves out on the street. *You don't realize how privileged you are*, they would lecture us, *what with so many perverts walking around out there, abusing young people*. They also warned that the state would punish with a firm hand those who squandered opportunities like ours and chose instead to leave the fold to commit criminal acts. Apparently, there were places far worse than our school, like detention centres, or the shelters on the outskirts of the city, *Full of kids who aren't like you,* whose parents had left them behind in their journey towards the border. All we had to do was behave badly and we would end up in one of these. Generally, after a sermon like this, the runaway would end up begging for forgiveness between sobs. As punishment they would be given three extra hours of community work, cleaning toilets or scrubbing the kitchen floor. Then everything would go back to normal. There were, however, a couple of exceptions. They looked for Tere Valdivia for more than six weeks and she never came back. Ernesto Miranda did, but that same night he hung himself by his regulation trousers in the back of the sports hall.

Parque Acacias, situated a block from my house, is the heart of this neighbourhood. I go for walks there on weekends and, when my schedule allows, before work. I know very well its trees, bushes and a few of its most devoted visitors, with whom I don't tend to exchange more than a couple of words, but whose movements I observe with curiosity; I know, too, the newspaper man, the ice lolly vendor and the street sweepers. I have visited all the cafés dotted around the edges, and in a couple of them, the waiters know what I'm going to have for breakfast without needing to take my order. That morning it wasn't particularly cold, but a light rain was falling over the city. A few drops dripped from the tops of the trees, and from the streetlamps, too. There were very few people in the park. I sat down at the terrace of Café Walsh, still thinking about the poster I had just seen. There were very few customers – a handful of older women, the sort who go out for breakfast every Saturday, whatever the weather; a father with two children, and Dr Lombardo – so I was served right away. Opposite me, a man was reading a newspaper on a bench. Every now and then he would lift up his nose as if trying to identify some scent in the air. He was wearing a brown wool jacket and a chequered scarf. He must have felt like he was being watched because all at once he looked up and smiled at me for a second and a half. It was a fleeting but moving expression, like those flashes of lightning that cross the sky and announce, without a sound, the arrival of the rain. This brief exchange told me all I needed to know: the guy was Manu, the man from the poster. I took a couple of sips of my coffee and, in an impulsive act, got up from my table. I left the Walsh and headed back to where I'd seen the poster. I took my phone out of my jacket pocket and dialled the number of the woman to let her know that I had found him. She answered immediately and when she heard what I said, she let out a sigh that wasn't exactly of relief.

'I don't know what to say. In the last week more than ten people have rung me, assuring me that they've seen him and, when I go to see, it's never him. How can I tell if you really have found my son?'

'The place where I saw him is close by. If you like, I can go back and ask him what his name is.'

'No! Please don't talk to him, I beg you,' replied the woman, becoming defensive. 'If it really is him, he'll probably just run off. He's scared of people, you see. The poor man's had some very difficult experiences and he's still fragile. He might even attack you.'

I was silent for a few seconds while I decided what to do. Then an idea occurred to me: I would go back to the café and, from my table, take a photograph of Manu.

'I'll text it to you and then you can judge for yourself.'

The woman agreed and thanked me, not before reminding me again of how many times people had filled her with false hope.

When I went back, my coffee was cold, and I asked the waiter to bring me another cup. When he did, I asked him to take a photograph of me, making sure that the face of the man sitting on the bench was very clear in the background. The trick was so good that Manu didn't even realize. After zooming in a little and cutting myself out,

I sent the picture to Mrs Carrillo's phone, and she replied immediately: *That's my son. I'm sure of it. I'm heading over there. Please just confirm that he's still in the park.*

I sent the woman my location, paid the bill so I would be ready to follow Manu in case he got up from the bench, and carried on casually drinking my americano, looking forward to the joyous encounter I was about to witness. Now, with hindsight, I think that I would have liked to talk to him, to hear his story and, above all, to interrogate him about his relationship with his mother, for few things intrigue me more than actual mothers, looking as they do so different to the idealized version I have always had of them. Had this happened, perhaps things would have taken a different turn, and I different decisions, ones that would have allowed me to feel better about myself. Rarely do we decide how we should act based on the present, and much less on the intuition of the moment. We do it based on the good or bad experiences that we have had before, and on the prejudices about reality that we form as a consequence of these.

Once I had him before me, I saw that something Mrs Carrillo had said about her son was true: Manu was a fragile man. All of his movements betrayed a great vulnerability, both physical and psychological, and yet, how different his expression was that Saturday from the one he displayed in the photograph. Far more serene now, you might say, or at least not as tormented. The bags under his eyes also seemed to have faded. Manu never got up from the bench. He stayed there, peaceful and unworried, even when a little boy stopped in front of him to eat a magnificent stick of candyfloss. He only moved slightly towards one end, trying to protect his newspaper from that explosion of fluorescent pink sugar. And so, in this almost bucolic tranquillity, around a quarter of an hour went by.

Then, from the corner of the park where the café is, I saw an ambulance pull up. Its siren wasn't going, which meant I almost didn't notice its arrival. Two nurses got out and headed in the direction of the park. One of them was carrying a medical bag. Almost immediately, an older woman appeared in a Mercedes-Benz. Without moving from the table, I saw how the men took hold of Manu as his eyes grew clouded with worry once more. I said to myself that, although he had a mother, his expression was exactly the same as that of all the orphans. Without putting up a fight, without even struggling with the men, he let them lead him over to the ambulance they had arrived in and shut him up inside it. The woman, however, did not get out of the car.

PLAYING WITH FIRE

'The devil can be a cloud, a shadow, a gust of wind that shakes the leaves. He can be the nightjar flying across the sky or a reflection on the surface of the river.'
— Liliana Colanzi

Things had started falling apart a month or two ago. Although it was no longer mandatory, the lockdown was driving us all mad. What's more, at around that time, a few unsettling events had taken place in our building. One morning, as I was about to take out the rubbish, I saw that someone had defaced our corridor with threatening, vulgar pictures. To call them 'graffiti' would be to confer too much value on them. They were ugly drawings, pretty rudimentary, made with chalk, permanent marker, even lipstick, but there was something violent about them, something that went beyond the crudeness of a pair of tits or some hairy genitals; probably the rage with which they had been executed. This rage entered my body and mingled with the indignation the incident triggered in me. I immediately went to find a cloth and a bottle of detergent and asked my sons to help me scrub them off. Two days later, the images appeared again, this time on our own front door.

'It has to be one of our neighbours,' said my husband.'People doing actual graffiti use aerosols and that kind of thing; and anyway, no one's going out onto the street at the moment.'

But this explanation scared me even more. The fact that some highly-strung neighbour had taken against us was just as or even more frightening.

Days later, all the windows in our apartment became

jammed, as if someone had locked them from the outside, and then miraculously started working again. One night, the kitchen tap turned itself on while we were sleeping and flooded the dining room floor. The next day, as I dragged a dishcloth over the tiles, I thought about my maternal grandmother, who used to interpret dreams where water and floods appeared as an unequivocal omen of death. Luckily this wasn't a dream but reality, a reality so inexplicable there was something dreamlike about it. Meanwhile, my husband kept trying to reassure me. He talked about crumbling window frames or neighbours with too much time on their hands, but I couldn't see any of these as random events with no connection between them. Whether it was in our apartment building, or in this infected world we almost never went out into, something pernicious seemed to be taking over our lives. This is what I told my husband as he looked at me with concern, at times even with pity.

'You're getting in your own way, Gabriela. You can't let these fears keep controlling you. Take a look back at history: there've been pandemics before. The drawings on the walls are being done by someone, and I don't think they're aimed at us.'

His words would calm me down for a few hours, but then later I would remember the drawings or hear sounds in the kitchen again, and my disquiet would return, stronger than ever.

The boys weren't doing so well, either. Bruno had started secondary school in the middle of the pandemic and had spent almost a year studying online, not mixing with any other children his age. The isolation combined with his hormonal changes were making him feel almost constantly impatient, something which was on occasion very tricky to manage. In order to protect himself from his older brother, Lucas adopted a low profile, behaving as discreetly as possible. Although neither boy had ever liked board games, my husband would propose games of Risk and Scrabble in the hope of luring them away from their screens. The idea for the trip was his.

'You'll see,' he assured me. 'A weekend of breathing clean air will be enough to make us all feel sane again. You'll come back feeling like a new woman.'

'Can we take our bikes?' asked Lucas, who hardly ever opened his mouth at this point, and this sudden burst of enthusiasm from him seemed like a good sign.

We bought a large rack to transport the bikes on the back of the car so we wouldn't have to dismantle them. Bruno, however, didn't seem too excited about the idea of spending a weekend in the woods. He has always been scared of insects and is disgusted by the thought of his hands getting muddy.

'You know I don't like the countryside,' he protested when we described our plan to him. 'Can't we go somewhere else?'

My husband was born in a village surrounded by mountains and his family owns a large nursery for flowering plants that we visit quite regularly. The fact that his first-born son rejects his rural roots is a personal affront to him, but this time he didn't say anything.

Two weeks later, we made our journey to Santa Elena, which in photos looks idyllic – an ancient forest surrounded by mountains – but turned out to be far less so than we would have wished.

The cabin we were staying in was small and functional, although not attractive. There was a large bed in the downstairs room, and a wooden mezzanine that was far too close to the ceiling. The kitchen and dining area were outside, and to get there you had to cross a little garden.

All this drew new complaints from Bruno. We, however, thought the accommodation adequate for three nights. In any case, the plan wasn't to be shut up inside for the whole day, but rather to go cycling through the forest or around the lake.

On the Friday morning we got onto our bikes, each carrying one element of the picnic in our rucksacks. It was hot in Santa Elena. It was the last week of April; the sun was at its peak in the sky, and the trees so dry they looked as if they were made of sand. As they moved along the dirt track, our wheels lifted up great clouds of dust. Shortly before we reached the start of the trail, we came across the lake. We stopped for a moment to get a good look at it. Bruno insisted we stay there for the remainder of the day, but the rest of us were keen to keep going and follow the route we'd found on the map, a relatively easy trail known as the Wizard of Oz.

'You go on ahead, then,' he insisted. 'I'll stay here and read until you get back. Just leave me my food.'

'We came here to spend time together and get some exercise,' his father replied. 'Aren't you bored of sitting around every day? Stop being so dramatic and pick up your bike.'

'I don't want to!' Bruno said. 'I hate the countryside. It's made for animals like you.'

His reaction surprised me. My husband's only response was to grab the book Bruno had in his hands and put it into his rucksack. Then he took him by the arm and pulled him up from the tree trunk where he'd been sitting. The poor boy could do nothing but obey and get back onto his bike.

'They really picked the right name for it!' Lucas exclaimed as soon as we reached the circuit. 'The path is completely yellow!'

Despite his good mood, I felt ill at ease. As well as believing in the symbolic power of dreams, my grandmother was convinced that natural spaces have invisible but powerful guardians, and that in the forest it is possible to spot them. *You must be respectful towards them*, she would warn me. *If you ignore them, they can turn against you*. I had never sensed these spirits, but as we cycled onto this trail it seemed to me that the ground, the rocks, the trees and the sky formed the extremities of a being whose consciousness was observing us.

We spent the next few minutes in silence, pedalling along the curves of a dirt track, a carpet of dry leaves and, on either side, endless lines of trees. Lucas and my husband were in front and I followed them watchfully, trying not to lose sight of Bruno who was several feet behind us, still moaning and going deliberately slowly. Having children is to always be waiting for someone.

Annoyed at his brother's behaviour, Lucas pedalled furiously off into the distance, not caring if anyone went with him or not. As in so many other instances, I felt torn between the demands of my two sons.

'You go with him if you like,' suggested my husband. 'I'll wait for Bruno.'

I had no choice but to pick up my pace and chase after Lucas, who was speeding ahead through the trees.

I had the dizzying impression that I was retracing my steps, not simply as if we had already gone around the same trail several times – which we most certainly had – but as if before, in a dream or a previous life, we had passed several times through this forest. This was what I was thinking when we came face to face with Bruno. He was walking along pushing his bike grumpily, as if it were an encumbrance.

'Where did you go?' I asked him. 'Your dad was waiting

for you. Didn't you see him?'

But Bruno didn't answer me. He kept walking, his mouth fixed in a pout. His eyes, darker than ever, were ringed with emerging bags.

'This place is full of creepy crawlies. Can we go home today?'

'We've rented the cabin for three nights, remember?'

'So? No one's going to stop us from leaving, are they?'

I knew that when he was in a bad mood it was best not to argue with him and instead to wait until he cheered up a bit. He was clearly tired and hungry, so I said nothing more.

It was difficult to decide which way to go. Bruno insisted that the way out of the forest was in the opposite direction to where his brother and I claimed. Less out of conviction and more so as not to antagonize him, Lucas and I decided to turn around and pedal back the way we had come. Ten minutes later, we found the main path and, sitting at the edge of it, my husband, with a hostile expression identical to the one Bruno wore. Although I adored my son, I thought it unfair that his bad mood should ruin our trip.

'I think we should just have lunch now,' said my husband, resignedly, taking a red and white picnic blanket out of his rucksack.

The place was utterly uninspiring and didn't seem like the best spot to have a picnic at all – nothing compared to the lake, the hills or the panoramic vista the viewpoint promised, but once again I chose not to say anything. I sat down on the ground, looked up at the sky, and let myself be mesmerized by the treetops.

Bruno went over to the rucksack, rummaged around in it impatiently until he found the flask of water and started taking frenzied gulps from it.

'Hey, you brute!' shouted my husband. 'Don't drink all the water! It's for everyone.'

Then, without anyone seeing it coming, Bruno spat his mouthful of water into his father's face, as if to justify the insult. Without even taking a minute to dry himself off, my husband began to run after him, one hand raised in the air. I carried on watching the dance of the trees for a little while longer, as Bruno's cries floated towards me from a distance.

'Help me, Mum! Don't let Dad hit me.'

I smiled with the same far-off feeling I had been experiencing up until then, certain that my husband would never dare do anything of the sort.

There was a long silence. I turned, intrigued to see what was happening, and saw that my husband was raining smacks down on our eldest son's behind. When he finished, he shook his hand as if trying to get the feeling back in it, and I realized he had hit him really hard. I gave him an incredulous, reproachful look, which he immediately dodged. Then, still frowning, but pretending everything was fine, he took the things from the rucksack and laid out our food on the picnic blanket. Bruno moved away from us, tears streaming down his face. Every two or three steps he kicked the dry leaves angrily.

When I saw the food, I felt myself retch in disgust. My stomach was a stone weighing heavily in the middle of my body.

'Why did you do that?' I asked, livid.

'The boy has no manners. Don't you get it?' my husband replied, his mouth full of bread. 'He needed to be punished.'

'You're the one who doesn't get it,' I protested. 'He's growing up. Can't you see his hormones are all over the place? If the pandemic has made us anxious, he's suffering three times as much. And the only thing you can think of is to humiliate him?'

My husband didn't reply. I breathed deeply, trying to calm myself down.

'Listen,' I said after a while. 'I think Bruno has lots of things he wants to tell us, and he doesn't know how.'

'Well instead of winding us up, perhaps he could write us a letter.'

'I've got lots of things to tell you, too,' Lucas piped up.

I stroked his head fondly and stood up, trying to figure out which direction his brother had gone in.

My boots sunk into the dry leaves as if into quicksand, but no matter how far I walked I could find no trace of my son. The trees all looked exactly the same, and so it was very hard to orientate yourself. All that was certain was that I'd moved quite far away from my family, because I could no longer hear the voices of Lucas and my husband, but nor could I hear Bruno's tears. I felt my chest contract with anguish once again. *Something bad is going to happen to him*, I remember thinking. As I walked, I asked the spirit of the forest to protect Bruno and to lead me to him. In exchange, I was prepared to pay any price, whether a part of my body or even my own life. I announced this clearly, with the voice in my mind, pretty sure that spirits tend to hold you to these kinds of rashly made promises.

It was then that I saw him, sitting a few feet away, sobbing. I crouched down beside him and encircled him with my arms, just as I have always done, ever since he was a little boy.

'It's alright,' I said. 'Everything's going to be OK.'

'I hate Dad.' His guttural voice was almost unrecognizable. 'I don't understand why you're still with him.'

As if my son were a tree oozing resin, I could feel the rage and sadness his body was emanating. I saw him as a being halfway between the boy he had been and the adult he was becoming.

'You're just going through a difficult period with him. You'll soon make up, you'll see.'

Bruno wiped his tears away and looked at me doubtfully.

'Now come on, let's go. You need to eat something. I brought your favourite chocolate bar.'

He resisted a little at first, but then in the end gave in, and we walked back together, very slowly, to where the other two were finishing off dessert. My husband's head was still bowed, and it seemed to me as if the bald spot on the crown of his head had grown a few inches in diameter. All four of us were silent. Because of this I was able to hear the wind whispering above us in a different language to our own, but one which didn't sound foreign at all. I put my hand in my rucksack and took out my packet of cigarettes. Then I moved off to smoke without bothering the others. I let the astringent taste of the tobacco flood every one of my taste buds, avoiding the disapproving glances my husband threw me every now and then.

Eating did Bruno good – I've always picked up on how his mood changes hugely depending on his blood sugar levels. His body was suppurating a little less unhappiness, and his scent returned to how it always was.

Lucas and my husband put the picnic leftovers in the rucksack and when they were finished, got back onto their bikes, but Bruno refused to cycle any more. I had to promise that I would walk back to the campsite with him so he would pick his bike up off the floor and agree to take it back to the cabin. The wind was no longer singing, and the sun beat down with less force.

When we got back, I took a shower and, when I'd finished, asked the boys to do the same. When we had all washed the dust from the trail from ourselves, we went out to play Scrabble at the picnic table in the garden. I remember that I drew the tile that meant I could go first, and that I felt a chill run down my spine when I saw the seven letters laid out on the little plastic rack: they formed the word S A T A N I C. I swallowed hard and the saliva got stuck in my throat. I moved the tiles around and spelled out S A I N T on the board, like someone throwing a few grains over their left shoulder after they have spilled salt, a move that gave me a lower score. Straight away I thought about my husband saying *You're getting in your own way. You can't let these fears keep controlling you.* Bruno has always been very good with words – he's top of his class in language and literature – and in Scrabble it's as if the letters obey him. The first word he put down was J O K E R, then he waited a couple of turns and added B A S T A R D, then B U L L Y, putting his tiles down on a part of the board that gave him a triple word score. At first we didn't notice, but then it started to become obvious that all these insults were aimed at his father. I know my husband and, although this time he said nothing, I could tell he was furious again. He must have felt trapped by this game, which he always loses, not because he doesn't have the vocabulary but because he's bad at spelling.

As soon as it grew dark, we went up to the area for making fires. In our rucksacks we had a barbecue and some food. Bruno collected firewood as instructed by his father, and then sat down on a rock to watch how his father and brother arranged the branches in a pyramid, leaving gaps around the bottom so the air could circulate. No one asked him to get involved and nor, as was to be expected, did he do so voluntarily. Perfectly in sync with his father, Lucas tended the fire the whole night, making me feel not just safe but proud, too, of his caution. At least one of us has a measured character, I remember thinking. After we'd eaten, Bruno and I gathered everything up and washed the dishes, humming Beatles songs as we did so. We all went to bed before ten, exhausted by the events of the day, but I was awoken in the middle of the night by someone tugging at my sleeve.

'Mum, can I stay here with you?'

I opened my eyes in surprise. It had been several years since Bruno had wanted to get into our bed.

'Is something wrong, sweetheart? Why aren't you asleep?'

'I'm scared. I don't feel right here.'

I turned to look at my husband, who was facing the stone wall of the cabin and snoring on the other side of the bed. I shunted gingerly over towards him, letting our son take up the space on the opposite edge of the mattress. Bruno curled up next to me and almost immediately fell asleep. A little while later, I was woken by my husband's indignant voice.

'Don't think you're going to stay here,' he said in a tone of voice that to me sounded unnecessarily strict.

'He had a nightmare,' I replied, defending the boy.

'Well, he can comfort himself. He's too old to be sleeping with his mummy.'

I didn't want to argue in front of the children, so there was nothing I could do but swallow down my anger. Bruno got out from under the covers without a word. I did the same and went with him up to the mezzanine. I lay down at his side and waited for him to fall asleep. When I went back to my bed, I wasn't sleepy any more. I spent a good while watching my husband's breathing as revealed by the movement of his back. Meanwhile, the images from the previous day came back to my mind like the pieces of a jigsaw puzzle: the arguments, Bruno spitting the water, his bottom being spanked, and finally the letters I had seen on the Scrabble board. I wondered who the forest spirit really was, who exactly I had asked for protection for my son. I got up and left the cabin and went to light a cigarette. There was no moon, but the stars weren't visible either. The sky was as dark as could be. I had only been outside for a minute or two when I heard Lucas' footsteps, careful and unmistakable, coming towards me.

'Mum? What are you doing?' he asked, in his sleepy little voice.

'Nothing, my love. I'm just out here, thinking.'

'About what?'

'About how sometimes I feel like destroying everything.'

Unlike his brother, who always tells me off whenever he sees me smoking, Lucas said nothing about the cigarette. He simply gave me a sweet, silent hug, and went back to bed without being told to.

In the morning, Bruno got up much later than usual. He appeared in the kitchen when breakfast was already ready.

'You've got a good radar,' I joked. 'I was about to serve yours up. The Nutella's over there, look.'

I indicated the jar as I placed a steaming pancake in front of him.

'How do you feel? Did you manage to sleep a bit more?'

He didn't reply. Just as his father was doing, Bruno stared fixedly at his plate. The two ate in silence while Lucas and I tried in vain to lighten things up by talking about football, one of the few interests the four of us shared.

'You boys need to clear the table and wash up,' said my husband when we'd finished eating. 'Today we're going to do a slightly longer route than the one we did yesterday. Don't forget to fill up your flasks with water.'

This time, not even Lucas looked keen. I imagined myself cycling along beside Bruno, doing everything I could to convince him to keep going a little longer. But my husband was not interested in our opinions. He took a roll of toilet paper from the cupboard and walked back towards the cabin, his steps resolute. As soon as they saw him go through the door, the boys ran off in the direction of the garden, indifferent to the order they had just been given. I must admit I was cheered by their apparent closeness. Quickly, I began washing the plates so their father wouldn't tell them off, until I heard Bruno's cries.

'Get away from there now!' he was saying desperately to Lucas. 'Can't you see it's burning?'

I came out of the kitchen and confirmed what I already feared: a fire was approaching my sons, one bush already blazing and, on the ground, dozens of tiny but incredibly fast flames, which seemed to be leaping all over the place. Instead of heeding his brother's words, Lucas was staring at them intently, almost enjoying it, as if he were watching a video online and not the first signs of a blaze, at the fleeting moment when it is still possible to put it out.

In the email we'd been sent with the site rules, we had been warned that the vegetation was very dry and thus highly flammable: *When putting out your fires, use water, not earth. If you do not do this, they can start up again*. I ran to the kitchen in search of the large jug we had brought with us to the campsite and started tipping water all over the burning bush, but it was too late. The flames had already reached the surrounding plants and the straw-like grass that covered the ground. The water vanished as soon as it touched this cracked earth like a thirsty tongue. *Please, please, please*, I repeated over and over again in a low voice to who knows whom, probably the guardians of the forest, so they would prevent what was about to happen. But instead of getting better, the situation spiralled into something much worse, and eventually I lost my cool.

'Help! Fire!' I called to alert people. 'The forest is burning!'

I called my husband's name, too, hoping that the distress in my voice would bring him running out of the bathroom, regardless of what he was doing in there. Two forest wardens appeared in the outdoor kitchen and ordered us to scrape together as much earth as we could, while one of the women who ran the site called for help on her radio. A few seconds later I saw that the flames had reached the tops of the huge tree outside the cabin and were leaping up the trunk of another that was even taller, filling the air with thick black smoke and making it very difficult to breathe. All the surrounding plants were burning, and the flames licking around the tops of the trees reached up to the sky. I took my sons by the hands and made them run to the car with me. Just at that moment, my husband appeared.

'The forest is on fire!' I told him. 'We have to get out of here.'

He took his precious time to understand what was happening, but eventually he reacted.

'You guys go if you want.' he said. 'I'm staying!'

Five men answered the radio call. In surprisingly organized fashion, as if this were a dance they had already practised several times, they formed a line while one of the forest wardens went along and handed each of them some kind of tool. As soon as they'd taken it, they entered the disaster zone, where the air was so dense it was impossible to follow their trail. My husband joined them without saying goodbye to us, disappearing into the pall of smoke like a zombie. I started the car's engine and prayed he would get out of there alive. I had nothing with me except for my two sons, my bag and my phone. A few feet off, I saw our bicycles carefully parked up against the cabin, the new helmets hanging from the handlebars. Everything else had been left inside.

In the back seat of the car, Bruno cried. I breathed deeply and put the car into reverse to get to the path that led out to the highway, but once on it couldn't help trying to spot my husband in the rearview mirror. The fire had reached the offices, and it wouldn't be long before it got to the cabin with all our things in it. A huge black cloud was spreading over the forest. The men who before had been running around hauling tools had disappeared into the smoke, and you could no longer make out a single human being.

'What's going to happen to Dad?' asked Lucas. His question moved me.

'I don't know, my love. Let's hope he doesn't put himself into too much danger.'

For the first time since seeing that burning bush, I asked myself how it had happened, and if they were in some way responsible. Or was it I who, when I asked for protection, had sacrificed the life of my husband in an utterly irresponsible manner? To banish this thought, I interrogated my sons. I did so bluntly and without hiding my annoyance, but they just sat there in silence.

'It was him,' wailed Bruno, eventually.

I thought that, yet again, he was trying to blame his brother for something he had done. It was practically a habit, but this time Lucas did not protest. He simply ignored us and turned his head to look back at Santa Elena. His attitude enraged me. More than ever, I needed certainties, not childish or pre-teen insolence, and so I stopped the car in the middle of the road to talk to them.

'Lucas, I want you to look at me. Is it true what your brother's saying?'

'Yes Mum, it was me,' he replied with that calm so typical of his; it seemed incongruent with everything that was happening. 'I set the bush on fire.'

'And look at this, too!' Bruno commanded me, grabbing his brother's arm roughly. On my youngest son's skin, I saw something drawn in pen, identical to the images that had appeared in our apartment building.

'He jammed the windows shut, too.'

I turned to face my eldest son in astonishment.

'You knew from the start Lucas was doing this and you didn't say anything?'

'I'm not the one you should be getting angry with!' he retorted.

I needed a break to think, so I got out of the car intending to light a cigarette, but no matter how much I rummaged around in my bag I couldn't find the packet. I locked the car doors to stop the boys from leaving and walked a few feet off. A group of local farmers rode past me on horseback. They must have been heading towards the blaze, towards the red and black clouds that had eclipsed the horizon. As I walked, I asked myself if I really knew these two boys whom I had given birth to and raised so carefully for years. I thought too about how unjust allegiances can be – how while I was capable of renouncing any aspect of my life for my children, they had pacts of solidarity that excluded me. Their father, meanwhile, had chosen to help the farmers and the trees rather than come with us. I felt no resentment towards him; on the contrary, I hoped he was safe and that this decision had earned him the goodwill of the spirits. Although my fears were screaming out to me to get back in the car and carry on driving towards the highway, this time I decided not to listen to them.

We returned to the campsite a couple of hours later, and the atmosphere we found was very different by then. The farmers had managed to make a firewall by sacrificing an extensive wall of trees around the blaze to control the situation, while the rescuers formed two human chains going in opposite directions to bring buckets of water to the edges of the forest and stop the hot embers from catching alight again.

My husband was one of the links in the chain. I struggled to recognize him since his legs, arms and face had turned the same colour as the trees. His features betrayed the exhaustion that had accumulated in his body; even his Crocs, warped by the heat, were now invested with a new and unwonted dignity. I went to greet him with a loving hug that surprised even me. Then I looked around for my sons and saw Lucas staring, a satisfied look on his face, at the wreckage of our bicycles and our weekend. The cabin, however, had remained untouched.

'Look, Mum,' exclaimed Lucas, pointing towards the doorway. 'Your cigarettes are still there.'

And it was true. All the things we had left out on the porch remained intact, as we had left them the previous night, but none of us were the same any longer.

THE PINK DOOR

In my sixty-three years of life, it has never occurred to me to hire the services of a prostitute. If anything, I was the one who, as a young man, exchanged sex for favours – such as a good meal and a warm bed – when I went backpacking around Europe. You might say that it was Lili, my wife, who planted the seed in my brain with a passing comment that triggered a long chain of thoughts and actions. One afternoon, as we were walking through our neighbourhood down one of the deserted little streets adjoining our own, Lili pointed out a new business, although in fact all that was there was a very narrow door the colour of pink bubble gum, with little blue and green hearts painted on it in pastel tones. It looked like the door of a teenage girl's bedroom. The afternoon was fading, illuminating the cobbled ground of the alley and its grey walls with a violet light, and making the colour of the door stand out with an unusual glow. I suppose it was this light that made us notice it.

'Have you seen what's over there?' remarked my wife, excited as a child. She had stood up on her tip toes to get a better look.

High up in the wall, two coquettish little windows were pushed open like sleepy eyelids. Rather than designed to allow someone to see the outside, their function seemed to be to provide ventilation while preventing passers-by from looking in. If you made an effort, however, it was possible to make out a few decorative objects that rendered the place even more perplexing. My wife pointed out the candelabra with beads of orange glass – or were they plastic? – hanging from the ceiling. On the wall, a long red balloon with a metallic sheen formed the word *Love* in English.

'What a strange little space!' remarked Lili, awakening in me the same curiosity she felt. 'Have you seen it before?'

'Never.'

'You're the one who always walks home down this street. I can't believe you've never noticed it before.'

'Well yeah, but it wasn't here before. It's appeared overnight. Maybe they only painted it yesterday,' I replied, prickling a little.

'If that was the case it would smell of fresh paint, no? Most likely it's been here for weeks and we just didn't notice.'

'Maybe it's the room of a girl who's just left home for the first time,' I hazarded, and I would have been content with that explanation if my wife hadn't counterattacked.

'I've never known any woman old enough to leave home who still has balloons in her bedroom,' she replied, very sure of herself. 'Isn't it more likely to belong to a prostitute, or her pimp?'

I, in contrast, am convinced that bad taste has no upper age limit, but I was tired and wanted to get home as quickly as possible, so I chose to agree.

'Don't you even think about showing your face here!' my wife said, half serious and half teasing, pointing her finger at me.

I pretended to have lost all interest in the matter, but in fact, quite the opposite occurred. Over that same week I thought about the place again on several occasions. When I least expected it, the little door would appear in my mind's eye, except that now it was ajar, as if inviting me to enter. One night I imagined that I poked my head around it, allowing me to glimpse the owner of that room: a female student, with soft, brown skin, who was sitting in her underwear touching up the nail varnish on her toes.

The image produced a movement between my legs so unusual in recent times that I couldn't help but feel surprised; the most potent erection I had had in years. By my side, her head buried in a pile of pillows, my wife snored on. I looked at my watch: it was twenty-five past midnight. I thought about sneaking out of the house and walking to Calle Mariposa, but almost immediately recalled Lili's voice categorically forbidding me to go near the premises. I wondered when the last time was that she and I had had sex and, no matter how hard I tried, I couldn't remember.

I would be lying if I said that Lili wasn't a controlling wife. Even since before we had got married, she always took charge of deciding each and every one of the important things related to our family life. She was the one who chose the suit and shoes I purchased for my wedding, the name of our daughter, and the houses we rented for the first few decades we were together. Once we had saved enough money to buy some land, she chose this neighbourhood and breezily directed the entire construction process. I'm not complaining – her tastes and mine were almost always compatible, and I must admit that for years, her decisive character saved me many a headache, but it's also true that it frequently made me feel a little steamrollered. My survival strategy consisted of occupying the grey areas, those interstices which escaped my wife's tentacles due to their insignificance. Things like choosing the brand of coffee we drank or how we separated the rubbish allowed me to preserve my dignity but weren't enough to amass sufficient quantities of enthusiasm for life, nor to diminish the resentment I felt for decades of not being master of my own destiny. Perhaps this is why, when I discovered the effect that place produced in me, I decided to ignore the ban on going near it and to push my rebellion as far as possible. It wasn't easy to maintain this conviction. Several times I walked down Calle Mariposa hoping to step across the threshold of that little door, but it was always closed. The windows, too, were also closed most of the time and the frosting made it impossible to make out what was happening inside. Nothing on that external wall stood out. The stones seemed sunk into their characteristic deep and lethargic sleep. Even the colour of the wood, I fancied, was duller, as if diluted.

It was on Thursday, 24 September – I remember it exactly because on that day Clara, our daughter, was going to turn thirty-one – when the first anomaly occurred. Clara was due to come round that evening to celebrate with us. I had called her first thing to say happy birthday, and we chatted casually for a few minutes. Then I spent several hours trying to focus on an insurance forecast I had to deliver to one of my clients. The work bored me, so I decided to get up from my desk. In the kitchen, I found my wife, who had started making the cake she baked for our daughter every year. She had run out of vanilla extract and asked me to go to the supermarket to get some. I made a face as usual to avoid her suspicion but, deep down, I was pleased to have a pretext to go out at that time of day.

The sun had begun to set, and Calle Mariposa had been painted violet once again. A man and a woman were chatting in front of the now open door. The woman had her back to me, so it was impossible to tell that much about her, except that she was slim and broad-hipped. She had straight black hair, gathered up under a red cap exactly the same colour as her blouse. The man was dressed in a similar fashion. They looked like they worked at a cinema or a chain of fast-food restaurants. From where I stood it was possible to get a glimpse of the room beyond: the orange candelabra was still dark, and next to the brick wall I thought I could make out the bed, which supported my wife's theory about the nature of the business. The man opened the boot of a car and began to unload several cardboard boxes, small ones, like the ones used for transporting books, although I thought it rather unlikely that this was what they contained. I didn't want them to see me loitering around, and so I turned and headed straight to the supermarket. I bought the vanilla extract and walked back as fast as I could. The man and the woman were no longer there, but the door was still half open. The light had been switched on in the room, and the metallic balloon hanging from the wall reflected those same glimmers of light I had seen the first time. The bed, meanwhile, had vanished. In its place was a sofa, and in front of this, a little coffee table.

'You can come in if you like,' said a voice so sweet I felt compelled to obey it. It was then that I saw there was someone sitting in the back of the room, in front of what must have been a wardrobe or, at most, the door to a bathroom. This person was dressed the same as the others: black trousers, a red top and a cap. It was impossible to make out their gender. On their lap, a box of sweets just like the ones brought around by the confectionery vendors in cinemas and theatres shortly before the show begins. What was this person doing there in work mode, as if there were customers to sell to? Their only potential buyer, at least at that moment, was me. For a second, I thought about asking once and for all what kind of place it was, but I didn't, probably because it seemed obvious that the sweets were a front and that asking would not only be awkward, but would put everyone involved on the defensive.

'I'm sorry, but my wife is waiting to make a birthday cake and I've already wasted a lot of time. She'll be annoyed by now, and if I don't go back home soon, she'll put me in the oven instead of the cake.'

My interlocutor lifted her gaze. She was a girl with her hair cut very short and large brown eyes, which she fixed on me imploringly.

'Take one of our sweets, at least – it'll sweeten your way back home,' she said, as softly as before, holding out a cellophane bag with a tiny little sweet inside it. 'It's a sample, I won't charge you for it.'

I didn't want to be rude, so I accepted her gift and popped it into my mouth. Immediately an aniseed flavour washed over my tongue. I like most sweets, but there are some flavours that drive me wild, and one of these is aniseed. As I savoured it, I walked rapidly, resigned to being ticked off by my wife.

I entered the house breathing hard to let her know that I had run all the way home, but instead of finding Lili at the stove, her apron covered in flour as I had left her almost forty minutes earlier, I saw her sitting on the sofa, absorbed in one of those comedies I find entertaining and which she never lets us watch. At first, I told myself that she had decided to do without the vanilla extract, but there was no smell of cake either, and in the kitchen not a trace that she had been baking.

'Sorry, darling,' I said with an artificially remorseful tone. 'The shop was really busy. What time is Clara getting here? Will you have enough time to finish off her birthday cake?'

Only then did my wife lift her gaze from the TV, a strange expression on her face.

'I think you've got mixed up,' she said, 'her birthday's a month away.'

I am an absent-minded man, and so would gladly have believed that this was a misunderstanding if we hadn't spent part of that afternoon planning the menu and going over the ingredients for her birthday dinner.

'Is today not the 24 September any more?' I said, flippantly.

'It is, but Clara's birthday is the 25 October. Don't you remember the date your own daughter was born?'

Of course I remembered. I had written it dozens of times on all kinds of official documents over the course of my life, and I was certain it wasn't in October.

I let Lili carry on watching her film and went up to the study to call Clara. In the background, I could hear the din of an airport at full volume, with that metallic voice calling passengers to start boarding, and it was clear she didn't have the slightest intention of coming over this evening.

'Can I call you in a couple of hours, Dad?'

She must have noticed bewilderment in the few words I managed to stammer out, because immediately she asked:

'Is something wrong? Is Mum alright?

'Everything's fine. I just wanted to say hi.'

The confusion remained with me for the rest of the night. As I tossed and turned, I wondered if I wasn't starting to suffer from some kind of dementia, which Lili insinuated on a regular basis, and whether I ought to go and see a neurologist.

I worked all next morning, trying not to think about anything that wasn't calculations and probabilities, but as soon as the heat grew less intense and the sky began to grow dark, I returned to Calle Mariposa, drawn by the mystery. The candelabra was already lit when I arrived and saw the half-open door. I had the feeling that someone was waiting for me. This time my feet stopped not at the entrance, but a few feet away. Another man was waiting by the door. He wasn't wearing a uniform. More than a cinema employee, he looked like any one of my neighbours. Before knocking at the door, he straightened his shirt collar and smoothed down his trousers. He was let in almost immediately. The street was deserted and so I plucked up the courage to go over, even putting my ear against the door. I managed to hear the vibrations of a dialogue I interpreted as intimate but perhaps was merely discreet. I didn't want to be seen spying out in front of this house, this room or whatever this place was, and so I started walking up and down the empty street. What did I hope to find exactly? This is what I asked myself as I wandered anxiously around the block. My wife's hypothesis had awoken in me a peculiar fascination, as well as the awareness of having longed, for many years, not just to disobey her but to do something truly transgressive. To go whoring, a few feet from my house, was without a doubt transgressive. But was this really what this business was? I wasn't convinced. If it was, I wasn't too sure I would dare to take it all the way, either. The mere possibility stirred up in me a mixture of fear and elation which I hadn't experienced in a very long time and this alone was already a bonus.

The man took a little over half an hour before emerging again, just when I had decided to leave. I carefully observed the happy expression on his face and felt a kind of envy – and simultaneously admiration – towards this individual, much bolder than I, who had been the first to pluck up the courage to resolve this enigma in our neighbourhood. It would probably have been enough just to intercept him and ask what he had discovered, but I wanted to see and hear it for myself, not via someone else. Once the street was empty again, I pushed at the door timidly, but without hesitating a single second.

'Come on in,' said a voice from inside. 'Feel free to take a seat. We were waiting for you.' I recognized the girl who had given me the tiny sweet.

Ever since I was a boy, my way of combating embarrassment has consisted of talking non-stop, and that evening I made full use of this tactic. I explained to the seller that I had waited a long time before deciding to come, that I wasn't in the habit of leaving the house, and that it had doubtless helped that they had opened this place so close to where I lived, where I worked from home as an independent contractor. I also said – and I regret this – that things with my wife had not been going well for a few years now, ever since she had retired, to be precise, and just stayed at home endlessly telling me what to do and what not to do. To conclude my long spiel, I assured the seller that I was in need of some kind of supplementary emotion, opening my eyes very wide to stress that this was innuendo. When I recall that day, it is all I can do not to blush and feel flooded by a profound nostalgia, because since then, my life has never been the same again.

'Don't worry, sir,' replied the young woman. 'We're here to help you with whatever you need. That's what we do.'

I thought that I would be led then and there to the back of the establishment or, in the worst-case scenario, that the girl would get up to close the door and start undressing without further ado. But she merely took out a folder of samples, samples of sweets.

'Pick one,' she suggested, flicking through the clear plastic pages of the collection.

With the same verbal diarrhoea I'd displayed before, I told her that the aniseed-flavoured sweet from the previous afternoon had been delicious and that I would happily eat another, except this time I would like it to be a little larger.

The saleswoman smiled at me, pleased. With her long, delicate fingers, she took a sweet from the folder and placed it in a little see-through bag.

'This time it's five hundred, Mr Moncada.'

I thought the amount excessive – it would have covered the service I'd been expecting from her, or, failing that, at least five packets of sweets from the supermarket – but my relationship with these people had barely begun and I didn't want to make a bad impression, so I tried to hide my surprise.

'What exactly does the price include?' I asked, as naturally as I could.

'The sweet and all its consequences,' the girl said, abruptly adopting a very serious air. 'Do you have any more family, Mr Moncada? Do you share your life with someone aside from your wife, is there another person who is very important to you?'

Only then did I become aware of all the information I had given this young woman about my private life, but it was one thing to be indiscreet and a different matter entirely for her to be asking me questions. I considered the possibility they might extort me.

'No. It's just me and her,' I replied, curtly.

As I sucked on the sweet, I thanked the saleswoman and hurried out of the place, minded never to return.

When I got home, my wife's car was not in the garage. The door to the kitchen, which we always left open, was locked that day. All the blinds were down and, even though it wasn't yet dark, the light on the porch was on. In the dining room, I found a note in Lili's handwriting: *I'll be in court till six. Back for dinner.* It had been years since my wife worked on a case, and even longer since she'd gone to court in person. My heart racing, I headed to the kitchen, took some fish and vegetables out of the fridge and began preparing them, as I had done for years, back when my wife worked outside the home, and which probably constituted the happiest period of my life. Two hours later, Lili returned. The tight-fitting skirt she was wearing looked perfect on her. The weight she had lost wasn't the only thing that struck me: she was wearing her hair long, too, and stylishly cut, with not a single grey hair on her head. She thanked me for dinner, poured herself the first of several glasses of wine and began talking animatedly about the trial and everyone involved in it that morning, taking it for granted that I was still interested in all these details and, sure enough – to my utter surprise – they did indeed interest me once again. Soon after, Lili came to sit on my lap and began to unbutton my shirt. I felt a desire for her even greater than the one she used to awaken in me when we first knew each other. As my lips slid along her neck, I told myself that five hundred pesos was really a laughably low price.

I remained like that for a week, enjoying the new situation intensely. Lili went to court in the mornings, and I would stay home on my own, working on my insurance forecasts in the study and then recouping territory in the rest of the house. In the evenings I would take great pains to prepare delicious dinners that always had a happy ending, whether in the living room or our bedroom. Who needed to think about hiring some strange woman when Lili was embodying the best possible version of herself? Though I had by now identified the source of all these changes, thinking about it was beyond me. So as not to worry about it, I decided to assume that life had always been like this, and that it would continue to be so indefinitely; that instead of going back to the little sweet shop that afternoon, I had woken from a long siesta and the years of unhappiness in my marriage had been nothing but a bad dream. My life with Lili was so harmonious at that point that I wonder if it wouldn't have been better to leave it that way forever.

By around the third week, I began to feel the lack of something that, at first, I struggled to identify.

'Have you heard from Clara?' I asked my wife one evening, just before dinner.

'Who's Clara?' she replied.

That night I couldn't cook. Trying to hide at least in part the anxiety eating me up inside, I left everything in the kitchen and, without even taking off my apron, went and shut myself up in my study. I searched unsuccessfully for my daughter's number on my phone. I couldn't find any photos of her, either. Refusing to believe it, I typed her full name into the search bar of my browser to try to find her, but it was futile. I recalled my conversation with the sweet seller, and chastised myself for not having told her the truth. By leaving Clara out of my story, she had erased her from my life. I had the sense that I had stupidly sacrificed the thing that mattered most to me in the world in exchange for a few years of marital bliss. I went to find a bottle of whiskey in the kitchen and sat weeping in rage and impotence for the rest of the night.

The following day, I went back to Calle Mariposa to ask them to give me my daughter back.

'That is completely beyond our capabilities, Mr Moncada, and even if we could do it, it wouldn't be fair to compensate you: it was your mistake. You concealed essential information from us when we requested it. If at any point you hire our services again, it is vital you tell us the truth. That way we can avoid this sort of issue.'

I strove as hard as I could to adapt to the life I had then,

I swear on my mother's grave, but my remorse was boundless. I cried all the time, and at any hour of the day or night, before my wife's astonished gaze. As if this weren't enough, I was fifty-seven years old, and Lili forty-one. Despite my efforts, I couldn't keep up with the rhythm she demanded of me. Every morning I would wake up exhausted with the sensation of having been bled dry. To reduce my exhaustion a little, I started ordering takeaways a couple of times a week. At around 6 p.m., I would call one of my wife's favourite restaurants: the Sicilian trattoria, or the Thai place on Encinos. At first she took it well, but after a month she began to worry about the expense.

'I work like a dog while you're at home. Can you not even take charge of dinner?'

Things grew worse when I rebelled against the obligation to fuck every day. As soon as she began snuggling up to me, I would move away and shut myself up in my study or switch on the TV. Lili made her bad mood and resentment abundantly clear. There was no end to her reproaches. One morning she even threatened to leave me.

'Fine then. Leave!' I replied, in a burst of honesty. 'Maybe I'll be able to live in peace then.'

But she didn't leave. She picked up her bag and her work files, climbed into her heels and left the house as if I hadn't said anything. That afternoon she returned from court hungry and with the same need for sex. We went on like that for several more weeks, in a tug-of-war between her needs and mine. It was as if, in spite of herself, my wife was tied to the house and to my body. My life had stopped being boring to become a hell on earth. I had no choice but to return to the little shop.

'How are you, Mr Moncada, sir? Is there anything I can do for you?'

The saleswoman greeted me with her customary benevolent air, but this time I found her attitude and the whole set-up almost unbearable.

Though I hadn't been invited to, I sat down on the sofa and then lay back on it disrespectfully. With no preamble, and without reciprocating any of her affected politeness, I told her at length about my domestic situation.

'There's too much of an age gap between me and my wife. We need the same levels of energy so we can understand each other,' I concluded. 'Can you not make both of us young?' I asked, sitting up.

The saleswoman looked into my eyes as if searching for some microscopic insect sheltering in the whorls of my irises.

'I could, Mr Moncada, but youth brings with it a great number of disadvantages. I'm not sure if you remember them.'

'And many advantages,' I replied. 'Including the possibility of starting over and correcting some of our mistakes.'

'Think hard about this, sir. Are you sure you want to do it? Coming back from there won't be so easy.'

Cockily, I accepted, not listening to her warnings.

This time the price was ten times as high. I paid with a bank transfer, expecting a proportional improvement in my life. It was the last time I saw my bank balance in good health. Devil-may-care, I swallowed the sweet down then and there and, when I stood up from the sofa, I felt coursing through my body a vigour I had not expected.

That evening, Lili and I were twenty years old and newly married. Like the other times, the date remained the same, as did the house, except now the furnishings were considerably shabbier. In the distance, I could hear the sound of a vacuum cleaner. In our little fridge I found a carton of eggs and a dozen beers. I opened one right away and sat down in the chair by the front door, my legs splayed open wide, in a posture I felt in keeping with the age I was now. I stayed like that for a few minutes, appreciating how good my eyesight was now. In the sky there wasn't a single cloud, and the sun flooded everything with a promising light. Soon after, Lili arrived, dressed in shorts and a top that exposed her back.

The urgent swelling between my legs was so intense it was hard to control.

'If you've finished sweeping the garage, do you think you could do the kitchen, too?' she said.

'If I've got to do something, I'd rather do you,' I replied, crassly.

My wife frowned.

'Have you taken some kind of drug without telling me? You're acting really strangely.'

'I haven't taken anything, sugar. Except a sweet they gave me in the shop on Calle Mariposa,' I replied, and began to laugh, surprised at my own brazenness.

'I asked you never to go near that place! Which part did you not understand?'

It was fascinating seeing how some of the things we had said or done in the future (I don't know how else to refer to the other times), were still applicable in this new time period.

'Don't be mad, babe! Those girls aren't like you imagine. They're wicked in a different way.'

Lili blew her fringe out of her eyes to signal her annoyance and picked up the hoover again.

'If you hurry up and finish your chores then maybe we'll have time to go and get something to eat in the market afterwards.'

I was moved by her suggestion. Forty-year-old Lili

would never have agreed to have lunch in a place like that, so scruffy and modest, yet so delicious. I told myself I'd made the right decision in going back to our origins as a couple, when there was still so much to salvage. I soon discovered, however, that it wasn't going to be easy.

In this new version, Lili was even more overbearing than in all the previous ones. As if this weren't enough, she had an especially strict approach to cleanliness. In order to approach her with erotic intent, I had first to shower and shave. Sex was a prize she bestowed on me when I obeyed her orders, or her constant demands, without arguing or putting up any kind of fight. And I needed her body just as before I had needed my anti-inflammatory medication and my sleeping pills. Now that we were newly-weds, her aim, apparently, was to instil a series of very clear, inviolable rules into our shared living situation: mine, meanwhile, was to correct all the stupid mistakes I had committed over the course of my previous lives. Once more we were stuck in a constant tug of war. I can't deny that on more than one occasion it went through my mind to return to the establishment to request another sweet, but I barely had enough money to cover half our rent. And even if I had been able to stretch to it, I'm not certain I would have opted to: anything that changes too quickly – a discovery that place afforded me – can also cause annoyance, a weariness one cannot live with.

One day, as I was walking down Calle Mariposa, I saw once again the uniformed salespeople unloading new cardboard boxes from a delivery van, and recalled that September afternoon when my wife and I had discovered that strange door. Where had Lili gone, the real Lili, the one with whom I had experienced all those years of happiness, misfortune and boredom, the mother of the daughter I had had for thirty-one years and whom I could no longer talk about with anyone? At that moment, despite all my reservations, I couldn't help but go in and beg the saleswoman to put us back to the way we had been at the start of it all, before she had changed the date of Clara's birthday.

'Nothing that's changed once can go back to being exactly how it was, Mr Moncada. You don't realize that each previous version is different to the way you remember it. I can try to make you old again, if that's really what you want, but who can guarantee that then you will like your life? I think it highly unlikely, to be quite honest.'

I explained to the saleswoman that, although my body was strong, I felt too mentally exhausted to be twenty years old. That at this point in my life I found it a real struggle to sleep on such a bad mattress, to eat pizza every three days, to spend my weekends in noisy nightclubs, and, worst of all, to lack the enthusiasm necessary to live for another four decades again.

'You have made a lot of changes in a very short period of time, sir. Let a few months go by. You'll get your energy back little by little, as you forget your history and your previous identity.' I felt a shiver and asked:

'And if that doesn't happen?'

'Then you can work for us. Being the witness to other people's lives is very entertaining, and far less tiring, you'll see. You can even move in here if you'd rather.'

This offer horrified me, and so I opted to cut the conversation short right away and closed the little door behind me, resolving never to set foot in the place again. I walked through a neighbourhood I barely recognized, feeling on my shoulders the weight of longing. Through the window of our house, I saw Lili engrossed in chopping vegetables. I stood looking at her for a few minutes, unable to decide whether the sensation of strangeness or familiarity that came over me was greater. The girl I saw there was not my wife but rather her prototype, but she was also – no matter how much or how little I liked it – the only thing that remained of her. When she saw me through the window, my wife smiled in surprise, put down her knife on the table, and went to open the door. Once inside, I clung to her waist and there, in the door to the kitchen, assured her that now I felt ready to start a family. That I would work hard so we never wanted for anything, and that we would always have vanilla extract in the cupboard.

A FOREST UNDER THE EARTH

In my parents' garden, there lived for many years a monkey-puzzle tree. Its colossal size for this piece of land gave it a somewhat monstrous, supernatural appearance. In some remote age, the house had belonged to my great grandparents, whom I never met, so the tree was already a feature in the black and white photographs Dad kept in a box in his study. Its leaves had always formed an important part of our family landscape and of my life. Perhaps for this reason, although also for its imposing presence, I saw it as the grandfather I had never known, or at any rate as a kind of protective, ancestral being. Trees like this live for over a thousand years. My father loved to say this, always in the same tone of wonderment. In reality no one knew exactly how old ours was, nor, of course, when or in what circumstances it had been planted, but Dad liked to think that this monkey-puzzle was the healthiest member of his family. According to him, it had far more time ahead of it than any of us did. The truth is, given that no one knew its age, I don't know how he was so certain about this. I have heard that one year in the life of a dog corresponds to seven of human existence; no one, however, has been able to tell me how to compare the age of a person with that of a tree like this. What is certain is that if there was one place in the world where I was able to feel safe, it was up in its branches. Ever since I was a very young girl, I learned to climb so high that no one could reach me. Sometimes when we visited a park or the gardens of family friends, I would try to climb other trees, but the experience was totally different: I could clearly feel their discomfort – their resistance, even – under the soles of my feet. My monkey-puzzle tree, however, always welcomed me. Whenever I felt unhappy, I would hide up in its highest branches and there I would find consolation. I wasn't the only one. Members of a diverse range of species would meet up there: birds, mainly, but also squirrels and stinging larvae, which, if your attention wandered even for a moment, would burn your skin with a red-hot acid. Each of these creatures had its habits and its needs. Some fed off the leaves, others the wood. To them the tree was a source of life; to me, an emotional crutch and a hiding place.

With my family, conversely, I was far less close. I exchanged barely a word with them all day, perhaps a few over breakfast or before going to bed. Each of us seemed to be living in a different film. Laura, my older sister, was the protagonist of a romantic comedy in which hairstyles and clothes were of paramount importance. Sergio, the middle child, seemed like a teenager in a Jim Jarmusch film, while my mother was one of Fellini's matrons: she was permanently exhausted if not in a bad mood. When she did speak to us it was to shout at Laura to turn down her music or to order me to go and have a shower. My father's film took place outside of the house, either in his office or one of his frequent social activities. Mine, in a private forest where no one, apart from me, ever dared to go. High up in the monkey-puzzle tree, I observed everything: the neighbours coming and going, my sister and her pathetic dance steps in front of the mirror, Sergio with his head buried in his computer for hours, and my parents shouting at each other in their bedroom. Seen from up there, everything that overwhelmed me seemed smaller, more ephemeral, insignificant, even.

Age poleaxes us all, it shuts off our senses. Perhaps this is why, as I grew older, I gradually distanced myself from my tree. School, my friends, the distractions of everyday life separated me from its branches. It's not that I had stopped needing it; rather that I didn't notice it any more. I no longer climbed its trunk, and my adventure film set in the forest transformed into a silent drama, shot mainly indoors, principally in my bedroom. From my bed or the living room sofa, I would stare at the monkey-puzzle tree without seeing it. Only occasionally, some visitor to the house – one of those female friends of Dad's, as short-lived as mushrooms in the rainy season – would make a comment about how beautiful it was, and then we would notice it, too. This outsider's gaze would allow us to marvel, to feel proud, even, as if having a monkey-puzzle tree at home was our own achievement and not some kindness from fate. I wasn't the only one who changed in those years. Laura finally began menstruating and going to parties, always accompanied by the same male friend. At home we were all so absorbed in ourselves that it took us a while to understand what was happening: the tree, seemingly so unchanging, had begun to age, too. The first thing I noticed was the absence of birds on its branches. I realized one morning before school that I couldn't hear them singing and I fell back asleep. When I looked out of the window, I saw in astonishment that its leaves, usually green and flexible like rubbery needles, were now a dull, indistinct brownish colour. I poked my hand out underneath the glass to touch them, and they fell to the ground, utterly withered. The trunk, once robust, had acquired a fragile, brittle appearance.

The insects were the only creatures that continued to frequent the monkey-puzzle as assiduously as before. Some even seemed to have proliferated. But this did not last long, either. One morning, as I left the house to go to my 8 a.m. class, I discovered a creepy crawly graveyard at the base of the tree. They looked as shrivelled as the trunk that had served to sustain them. I left my rucksack on the ground and set to giving them a decent burial, first beneath a layer of damp topsoil, then some gravel and a few bigger stones. I gathered up my books and headed off so that I would at least make the 10 a.m. class. After dinner, as the Channel 40 news was being broadcast on the TV, my brother asked me about the tree. He wanted to know how long it had been like this for, and what all the insects I had found in the garden looked like.

'You shouldn't have covered them with earth,' he said. 'Now we can't catalogue them and find out if one of them is the reason the tree's like this.'

I began to describe the victims to him as best I could, one by one, mentioning their colour, shape and size, what they had looked like before and after they were dead. Sergio wrote it all down in a notebook. Laura and Dad listened to the conversation in silence. We sat around the kitchen table and speculated for over an hour, until Mum's voice boomed out from the bottom of the stairs, informing us that it was 11.30 p.m.

On Saturday my father decided to call an expert. It was the first time, as far as I recall, that a gardener had been to our house. We all came out to greet him. As soon as he entered the garden, the man examined the monkey-puzzle tree from top to bottom. He bent down and, with a little metal rod, tapped the roots and the base of the trunk where large quantities of a thick, whitish resin were oozing out. There was something harrowing about this thick liquid, as if it were tears or a cry for help. The gardener cut off a leaf, folded it in half, looked at it closely and sniffed it several times before pronouncing his verdict.

'It's practically dead. It's going to be hard to save it.'

Despite our insistence, he was not able to explain the source of the disease, nor to give us any kind of advice to fight it. He took his fee and left leaving us perplexed and at our wits' end. That night I couldn't sleep and went to hide out in my brother's bedroom. Sergio showed me a piece of paper on which he had printed out images of some insects just like the ones I had described to him, along with others I had never seen. Underneath the images their names appeared in Latin. He told me that the velvety beetles were called *Nemonychidae*, the ones with a little snout, *Curculionidae*, and the copper-coloured caterpillars, *Lepidoptera psychidae*.

'They're all species that are symbiotic with monkey-puzzle trees. They exist across the whole continent. I don't think these are the creatures making it ill.'

For over a month, we observed the tree's decay without knowing what to do. I would like to say we tried hard to save it, but it wouldn't be true. What we did, chiefly, was to bemoan the situation and speculate about possible blights and parasites we had no idea about. My brother continued to investigate online without finding anything compelling. It was April, and the nights were so warm it was hard to fall asleep. Even so, I avoided opening my window to stop the stench of rotting from coming in. Instead, I would leave my bed and go downstairs to the living room where the temperature was more bearable. Once, I found my father reading on the sofa. In front of him on the coffee table there was a large pile of notebooks stacked up. I sat down next to him without a sound so as not to interrupt him. When he saw me, he put a hand on my leg.

'These are your grandfather's diaries,' he explained, looking directly into my eyes. 'I'm trying to find out if he ever saw the tree ill, too.'

'The gardener said it was almost dead,' I reminded him, fearful I would make him even sadder.

'That man knows nothing. All living things get ill from time to time. It's normal that one that's destined to live for centuries will suffer at some point in its life, don't you reckon?'

The months went by, and the tree became as shrivelled and lugubrious as the ones that appear in *Nosferatu*. It was then that the matter went beyond the limits of our family. The neighbours started talking of how dangerous it was to keep it there, listing all the possible scenarios. They said that, even if internally it was just a carcass, at its centre there was a terrible infestation lying in wait, which could spread to all the plants in the neighbourhood. As if that weren't enough, it was situated opposite a streetlight: if at some point it fell down, the dry wood could start a fire. One afternoon, Mrs Meyer, our next-door neighbour, came and knocked at our door. She was a very pleasant woman, and so my mother – who most certainly wasn't – showed her into the dining room where Laura was finishing some drawing homework. As she took sorrowful little sips of her chamomile tea, Mrs Meyer began talking about the monkey-puzzle tree. After beating around the bush for a while, she at last came clean and requested, straight out, that we chop it down. We were stunned.

'If you don't cut it down, this tree is going to fall and destroy all our houses,' she said, in the tone of someone trying to get you on their side. But it was in vain.

My mother was furious. Cursing, she kicked the neighbour out and told her, as Laura opened the door, that they would have to kill her – my mother – first before they could chop down the monkey-puzzle. It would stay there for as long as we lived in this house, and moving was the last thing we planned to do. Mrs Meyer must have assembled a committee of neighbours because from that day forth, someone would call at our house every afternoon to insist upon the topic, until we stopped opening the door.

One Saturday, my father came home with a couple of

sun loungers and a set of garden table and chairs, which he set up near the tree. The following week, he invited a couple of friends round. My brother got the barbecue out and helped Dad roast the meat, in the same place where weeks earlier I had buried the insects (it was impossible not to think of them when I saw the sweetbreads and chicken livers cooking on the coals). Even my mother agreed to come down for a few minutes and join the guests. That day my family began the custom of eating in the garden on weekends. My father would cook, as Laura came in and out with trays of snacks that I would help prepare in the kitchen. Again and again, we would drink to the tree's long life, surrendered to a kind of longevity ritual, which surprised our guests. We were all trying as hard as we could, and I'm sure that more than one person left thinking we were a united family. Only occasionally would one of them venture to ask if it wasn't dangerous to live so close to such a dry tree trunk. Whenever this occurred, the names of these people would immediately go down on our blacklist. Even among each other, it was prohibited to speak ill of the monkey-puzzle. We carefully monitored the number of green leaves on its branches, as if they were the vital signs of someone with a terminal illness hoping for a miraculous recovery. Very rarely would new leaves appear. The quantity of dead ones was far greater. Every night I would fall asleep with my eyes fixed on the window. In my head, the voice of Mrs Meyer repeating over and over again her diagnosis of putrefaction.

When autumn arrived, we stopped raising our glasses beneath the monkey-puzzle. The resin diminished with the cold, but now the wood creaked every time the wind blew or the temperature dropped, and these groans went deep into our souls. It was from that point on that we began to avoid going close to it, and to keep away from the part of the house that was threatened by the listing trunk. Without actually agreeing on it, we established alternative routes to get around, routes that corresponded to our own, unconfessed predictions about where the tree might fall on the day that it did finally come crashing down. One night Sergio took the computer from the study up to his bedroom. No one admonished him. Another day, my mother packed up the best dinner service which for years she had kept in the parlour, and put it in the back of the kitchen cupboard. And I moved my bed into Laura's room, where without complaint she gave me two drawers in her wardrobe so I could keep my important things there. Hardly any of us went out into the garden now, where the cold had taken control of the territory. This was why I was so surprised the night I found my brother sleeping out on one of the abandoned sun loungers by the monkey-puzzle tree. The moonlight gave his grey suede jacket a dangerous, attractive look, like the hide of a young werewolf. Sergio signalled for me to come over; I lay down beside him. He put his arm around my shoulders and asked if I felt sad about the tree. I nodded.

'Me too,' he said. 'But I'm glad you've come down. I've not seen you here before. The monkey-puzzle didn't want to let go of you.'

His comment made me feel even sadder. That night my brother told me that trees as tall as ours take years to put out shoots above the earth. Before they do so, they make sure that their roots are deep and strong enough to sustain them.

'The *roots*,' he stressed, his tone serious, 'that part hidden beneath the soil that nobody thinks about and that nobody wants to see – that's the part that sustains us all.'

I asked him if he knew what had happened to the tree. Sergio took a moment before replying. He said it was probably a fungus, an invisible parasite that got in via the soil and was poisoning our tree with incredible speed. He told me that years ago, one such parasite had killed off an entire forest in New Zealand.

'I don't think it's possible to cure it. It's dry all the way through. But don't be fooled: the tree's not completely dead yet.'

He must have seen my sceptical expression, because he immediately started talking again about that infinite network that spreads out beneath the soil of the whole continent, and of which our own tree formed a part.

'The roots are connected down where we can't see them. A tree isn't just one tree, it's also its entire species. And then there are the seeds – dropped and dispersed far and wide for so many years – which are now reproducing.'

As my brother spoke, I gradually drifted off. I later found out it was only for a few minutes, but it was enough time for me to have a long dream about what I had heard him say: the roots of the monkey-puzzle spreading out along the passages and the rooms in our house, the bodies of all my family members, including those of my grandparents. They entered through the soles of my feet and went up along my legs and torso, and then came out again through my eyes and mouth. They formed an intricate labyrinth, invisible but real, a kind of subterranean forest that connected us all.

I was woken by the sound of leaves being blown by the wind. It was very cold now, and there was an unusually strong breeze. I felt my brother's suede jacket covering me. Sergio and I got up from the lounger, our arms and legs stiff, and went and settled down in the living room where Laura had lit the fire. That night there was a storm with strong winds that lasted for over ten hours. Shut up in their room, my parents argued. From time to time, we heard the sound of something being thrown against the wall or of someone kicking the wardrobe door. This time, however, the row was overshadowed by the racket made by the hurricane. The news, which my siblings and I followed live on Sergio's phone, brought reports of the havoc being wreaked across the different neighbourhoods in the city. By nightfall there were reports of more than thirty trees having been brought down. Two streetlights fell a few feet from us, on Avenida Miguel Ángel de Quevedo. During this whole time, we watched our monkey-puzzle resist, displaying a dignity I had never appreciated before. In the morning, the sky was completely clear. As soon as I opened my eyes, I ran out into the garden to check on the state of things. I found my father sitting on the steps outside the door, his head between his knees. His eyes were bloodshot and his expression grave. Had he spent the night out here, waiting for the tree to fall down? I couldn't even bring myself to say good morning to him. In the end, he broke the silence.

'I always felt as if this tree was the one that kept our family together. Now that it's like this, I'm scared about what's going to happen with us,' he said, giving me a sad, questioning look.

All that remains of our tree these days is a piece of hollow trunk in the middle of the garden. Over the next few months, it gradually lost its leaves and its branches, but it never did fall down, as the neighbours had prophesized. Last year, Laura started studying at a design school in Italy, and moved to live there with her boyfriend. Sergio left high school to study gardening. He is still obsessed with monkey-puzzle trees, and says that at some point he will go to see the ones in Chile and New Zealand. He is saving up to do this. There are times when I too would like to go somewhere far away, to escape from the house, from my parents and the hollowed-out trunk, but I don't even attempt it. I'm sure that, no matter how hard I try, it would be impossible. The roots tying me to this house grow stronger and further-reaching every day and, although I cannot see them, I feel them holding fast inside me.

LIFE ELSEWHERE

It happened a couple of years ago, when my wife and I were renting the apartment. We had gone with an agency recommended by a friend and which charged very reasonable commission rates. After visiting apartment buildings in every neighbourhood of Barcelona, we selected two: one on Calle Mistral, near Plaza de España, and another on Calle Carolines, in the heart of Gràcia. The one on Mistral was a bright space, with a covered sun terrace that Anna immediately envisaged full of plants, like an indoor garden. The architecture wasn't especially lovely. It was one of those seventies buildings, squat and not particularly attractive, which this area is full of, but which to my wife seemed spacious and, as such, appealing. In contrast, the flat in Gràcia was on the first and grandest floor, on the left-hand side of Calle Carolines, coming from the Fontana metro stop. The building was old with good quality finishes. The wooden lift that went with the modernist main door and the columns and arches inside the apartment all gave it a certain air of distinction. In short, it was a very stylish apartment, somewhere you could host pleasant dinner parties – a home to be proud of. Unfortunately, it was somewhat gloomy, the sun only entering through the front part of the space. The light from the inner courtyard no doubt illuminated the apartments on the uppermost floors, but it failed to reach this one. This was the reason we didn't choose it right away. In her spare time, Anna did illustrations for children's books and preferred to have a bright space. I turned the matter over in my mind that weekend and eventually decided on the flat in Gràcia. Who cared about the lack of sun if we only ever invited people round in the evenings? In any case, Anna drew so infrequently that this sideline of hers shouldn't restrict us. When she did do so, she could use one of those artist's lamps that simulates daylight perfectly. I promised her that I personally would take charge of setting it up.

On Monday morning, we called the agency to let them know we had decided on the apartment on Carolines, but the agent told us it was no longer available.

'It's very much spoken for, I'm afraid. A young couple with two kids has reserved it.'

'We've already filled out all the forms,' I argued, to no avail. 'Can't you just rent it to us?'

But the man said it wasn't possible. The couple had already paid the deposit, and this would mean going against the agency's policy.

'If anything changes or they take too long to bring me the paperwork, I'll let you know right away,' he promised before hanging up.

That same afternoon, Anna went by the agency to pay the deposit for Calle Mistral. I, meanwhile, continued to imagine my life in Gràcia: the walks I would take around the neighbourhood, the films I would see at the Verdi cinema, the coffees I would drink out on the terraces, the old Teatre Lliure. I was convinced that living near the theatre would help me get back to it. Before the year was up, I would be working on some play or other. And so, as I thought about the future I wished I had, the Gràcia apartment became more and more essential in my eyes. On Thursday, however, the agency called me to confirm that it had now been let. There was nothing for it but for us to move to the one near Plaza de España.

Over July, Anna and I focused on renovating our new place. We painted the walls and the ceiling, arranged the wardrobes and planted the little inside garden she had imagined. When we'd finished, we decided to spend a few days away in my parents' village. When we came back from the countryside, the smell of paint had gone. Nonetheless, from the first night, I had the impression that the place remained uninhabitable. I had no reason to think so, and so I chose not to say anything to Anna. She, however, was happy with the results of the changes we'd made and of the colours we'd painted the living room.

That autumn, I devised a new strategy to get back into acting. It consisted of spending time around the youngsters who probably still had a degree of respect for actors of my generation. And so I organized various dinners in order to meet a couple of directors. I had been working for more than two years in one of the Generalitat's ministries, and three without setting foot on a stage. According to Anna, I should thank heaven for this crappy job and leave acting to my spare time, as she did with her illustrating. Our dinner guests would congratulate us on the apartment, but never offered me any work in their plays, not even as an assistant set designer. Winter was approaching, and the situation remained the same. As time went on, I was overwhelmed by an undefinable sensation, too serene to be called anxiety, but unpleasant enough not to go unnoticed. I suspected that something was brewing, something I couldn't quite see but which concerned me absolutely. I began to take walks in the afternoons to calm myself down. After work, I would roam the city with no particular route in mind. These walks would often culminate in me circling around the gravitational pull of a theatre. The Romea, if I was in El Raval, or the Lliure de Montjuïc, a little closer to home. Most of the time I didn't even go up to the entrance to look at the hoardings, but simply stayed on the surrounding streets waiting for people to leave after the performance and spill out towards the local bars and restaurants. It was enough for me to breathe in the intensity given off by the audience after a good show, this intensity I had felt so many times myself and which, as a teenager, had led me to believe that I was born to act.

It was one of these walks that took me back to Calle Carolines again. Ever since we'd finished doing up the place on Mistral, I thought a lot less about the other apartment. The place in Gràcia now formed part of that endless list of longed-for things that had never come to pass, and to which I believed I had resigned myself. Even so, once I was near Fontana metro station, I couldn't stop myself from going to have a look at the building. The street was quite dark. From the corner, I could make out the lighted windows on the first floor. When I got a little closer, I could hear music echoing. I noticed that there was a standing lamp just in the spot I had planned to put one, and I also fancied I could see a couple of pot plants. I stayed there for a few minutes, imagining that the silhouettes I could make out in the window were my own and those of my family. Not mine and Anna's, but a different family, a wife and children I did not know but who inspired a tenderness in me that was both profound and unbearably sad, like that inspired by loved ones we no longer see.

When I got home, Anna had made dinner and was waiting for me in the dining room, reading. I went to wash my hands and, when I looked in the mirror, I felt like another individual had taken over my face. I thought about the other house for the rest of the night. I couldn't let go of the idea that this apartment was the one most suited to my tastes and my way of being, in the same way as the one on Mistral was more appropriate for Anna. To console myself, I told myself that an apartment is similar in many ways to a child in whom the genes of two families are mixed. In our case, my wife's tastes had triumphed; perhaps it would be my turn the next time we moved.

That Friday, when I left the office, I headed once again to the building. It was the time of year when it started to get dark early, and so it was already night when I got off the metro at Fontana. This time, however, there were no lights on in the apartment. Almost all the windows in the property were shut. *That's normal*, I thought, *no one's home at this time*. And so I decided to take a seat in the café on the other side of the road. I chose a table near the street and ordered a decaf café con leche. The place had all the style of Gràcia's shabby little bars, Parisianesque and bohemian, with low lighting and a few posters on the walls. I saw that one of the posters was the listings for Gràcia's Lliure Theatre. They were putting on *Ubu Roi* again, with Alfred Jarry's character relocated to the political context of Catalonia. The play was going to run for the whole of the winter season. Although I had heard good things about it on several occasions, I had chosen not to go and see it. Xavi Mestre, a dark, muscular guy who played the lead, had been a classmate of mine at drama school. After graduation, Xavi had travelled to Italy and then Denmark to train with Eugenio Barba. When he returned, the Catalan theatre world embraced him like a Messiah, giving him the roles that up until then no one of our generation had managed to bag. As I sipped my coffee slowly, my gaze moved between the theatre listings and the entrance to the building opposite. Two places which had denied me access, except as a spectator.

This was where my mind was when I saw a woman stop in front of the property. She can't have been much older than thirty. She was slim and blonde, with her hair tied up in a casual but elegant style. A pram and a small boy were waiting for her to open the door. The face I observed for a second or two seemed attractive to me. A few minutes later, the lights went on in the first-floor apartment. The boy's silhouette appeared in the window and, a little further in, the woman with the baby in her arms. The warm atmosphere of the place spilled out towards the café on the corner. I carried on watching for a few minutes, then paid for my coffee and went home. This time, Anna had already eaten, and I found her in bed watching TV.

On Monday, we got up at the same time as usual. We ate a calm breakfast and left the house in opposite directions. But instead of taking the metro towards work, I sat on the green line like a zombie until I got to Fontana. I had to wait an hour in the café before I saw the first-floor tenant emerge. Judging by the little boy's outfit, it looked like she was taking him to school. I left a few coins on the table and prepared to follow her.

That week I called in sick to the office pretending to have the flu, and for five days in a row, focused on trailing the woman through the streets of Gràcia. Three days were enough to get to know her habits and schedule: after dropping the boy off, she would go back home and feed the baby in the living room armchair until ten. Later, she would take the pram out to Plaza de la Virreina, where she would sit and read in a café until it was time for lunch. Then she picked the little boy up from school and went back home. She hardly ever went out in the afternoons.

The rest of my time – that is, the hours not devoted to my espionage work – seemed trivial to me. My own life was comparable to those adverts on TV that interrupt a thrilling film. There was nothing I could do about this, except patiently to put up with it. Anna began making sarcastic comments, saying that these days I was on another planet. But I always told her it was to do with my professional dilemma.

On Thursday morning, when I left the house to head to the metro station, I was almost run over by a rubbish truck, and they never even drive particularly fast. I told myself that my wife was right: I ought to stop this nonsense and focus on work, but I wasn't entirely convinced by this, just as I wasn't entirely convinced by living on a street full of bureaucrats and immigrants, covered in dog mess, or by the graffiti on the walls of the metro. I wasn't convinced by the thick Barcelona accent my colleagues at work had, nor by way the cortados tasted in the coffee shop on the corner. Our neighbourhood wasn't bad, the building wasn't bad, and nor was the apartment; but no matter how much I looked around me, I struggled to see anything that was good. Life seemed unjust to me in every aspect. Being a trained actor, I could feign the same conformity my neighbours exuded, but I couldn't stop asking myself in which year or at what turning had I got off the highway that led to the destiny which, as far as I thought, was the right one for me, or, conversely, which corner should I have turned so as not to end up on this street crammed with cars, this high-speed avenue that led towards the frustrated parks of one's forties. My intuition told me that something good was waiting for me in the apartment we hadn't rented. Something unusual and refreshing, like a new start after several years of unhappiness.

As the days went by, I became less resigned to the role of observer and my discretion began to feel unbearable. I wanted to talk to the woman, gain her trust and get her to invite me to her house. I couldn't wait any longer, and so that Thursday morning I decided to intercept her in the café on La Virreina.

It was a sunny winter morning, one of those when it's not too cold and it's nice to sit outside on the terrace of a café. She took off her coat and ordered a coffee. Sitting a couple of tables away from her, I felt how the beating of my heart sped up. Even so, I blurted out my question bluntly, quite naturally:

'You were at the Institut del Teatre, weren't you?

The woman looked up. Her blue eyes stared hard at me for a few seconds.

'No,' she replied, with a foreign accent I struggled to place. 'But my husband was.'

We chatted for a few minutes. She told me she was Danish and had studied set design in Copenhagen until deciding to move to Barcelona to marry a man who was an actor. Before she even uttered her husband's surname, I realized I was talking to Mestre's wife.

'Don't tell me you're married to Xavi,' I said, feigning amazement.

I pretended to show a genuine interest in my ex-classmate's career; I recalled aloud the three student anecdotes in which he and I had crossed paths, shamelessly amplifying the significance of our relationship. She seemed charmed and listened attentively for as long as her maternal duties allowed before she had to rush off to her son's school.

'It's so rare to meet anyone from that time. Xavi's classmates hardly ever come to his shows. We should get together another day,' she said as she got up. She gave me a card with her name on it, her address on Calle Carolines, and a phone number. She was called Josephina and used her married surname.

I went home and put the card in a drawer. I didn't have the slightest intention of calling her, nor of following her around any longer. Things did not end there, however.

Three weeks later, Anna rang to tell me that Xavi Mestre had called the house that afternoon.

'He wants us to go for dinner at his place!' she announced incredulously, as if, instead of this, I had been nominated for an Oscar.

'And what did you say?' I asked fearfully.

'I told him Friday would be perfect. And I bet you can't guess which street they live on!'

'Actually I can. They were the ones who beat us to the apartment,' I replied, trying to see if Anna would help me out by hating them a little bit; I had forgotten that she had always preferred our apartment.

Even though we had never been friends, Xavi behaved as if he really was pleased to see me. The dinner was delicious, and the apartment looked even lovelier than a few months ago, when the agency had shown it to us. I found Mestre to be much changed, grown older and scrawny, more like the king Ubu than the boy I had known twenty years ago. I wondered if he was ill or if his appearance was the result of being in such a long-running play. Rather than making him pitiful, however, this premature old age just accentuated his air of superiority. Over dinner, he assured me that none of his classmates from the Institut del Teatre had wanted anything to do with him since he had returned to Spain. But despite his fellow actors all giving him the cold shoulder, not one director had ever put his talent into any doubt.

'It's no surprise all those second-rate actors hate you,' I said to indulge him. 'They're bound to be jealous...' I added, earning his sympathy on the spot.

During dinner, I got up twice to go to the toilet, and so was able to inspect the other rooms in the house, all as sumptuously decorated as the living room. In the hallway there were framed photos of Xavi onstage, as well as a commemorative plaque. All the furniture and other objects seemed familiar to me, and so I felt a sense of belonging that was hard to bear. This house was almost mine, but for some incomprehensible reason I couldn't live there.

When the night was almost over, Mestre asked me why I had stopped acting. I was about to tell him what I always reply, that is, that I prefer to have a stable, secure life with a nice apartment where the children I will have with Anna will be able to live, but I didn't dare. I shrugged my shoulders and, to my surprise, replied that I couldn't bear the arts scene, so full of rancour, bitchiness and scandal, and so had chosen to step away. He assured me that he understood perfectly.

It was a strange evening. We talked a lot about our studies, the dreams we had had, the path each one of us had chosen. Xavi described the play to me and his relationship with Catalan theatre, which wasn't as good as I had imagined. I was surprised by how honest he was with me. In his voice I detected a certain bitterness that at the time I couldn't figure out.

We talked and drank until the early hours. We promised to stay in touch, and Anna and I said we would have them to dinner next time. I don't remember exactly how we got home. When I woke up, my pounding head was a putrid swamp. Anna was staring hard at me. An hour or so later, she accused me of having designs on Mestre's wife. She asked me not to see her again. Even so, I rang that evening to thank them for dinner. Josephina answered the phone, explaining that Xavi was ill and refusing to let me speak to him.

'In general he's managing it quite well,' she had said. 'But today he couldn't even get out of bed.'

Her voice worried me. For the next few days, I couldn't

get Josephina out of my head. I couldn't tell if what attracted me to her was her personality and her mouth, or if my fascination was because she was married to Xavi Mestre, a man I envied everything about, including his contentious relationship with Catalan theatre.

That December was the coldest I can remember. The humidity got into our bones and Anna was still upset. I went back to the apartment on Carolines several times, although without her. I recall those visits to Xavi Mestre as the only interesting thing I did that winter. We would drink orujo and play chess in his study, where the sunlight hardly ever entered. During these games, he would grow distracted remembering our shared past at drama school. I couldn't believe that, after having been so successful, he felt nostalgic for that miserable period.

One afternoon, as we sat there sipping our drinks, he announced that he wasn't going to finish the run of *Ubu*. When I asked him why, he showed me a letter with the logo of a private clinic on it.

'My doctor insists I need complete rest, so I asked Rigola to postpone the show, but the damned idiot wants to find an actor to replace me instead. Can you believe it?'

In the next room, the little boy started shouting. When I asked Xavi what he planned to do about it, he replied:

'I'll think of something.'

I came downstairs, surprised at his answer. As ill as he was, the man still brimmed with self-confidence. As I left the apartment block, I ran into Josephina. She was waiting for me in the same café where I had spied on her apartment so many times. Her eyes were swollen.

I sat down with her at a table in the back. She spoke in a low voice, as if worried the other customers might hear what she was going to say. She explained the seriousness of the latest results to me. According to her, Xavi's illness was the consequence of several years of work without a break, but he was stubborn as well as selfish. She also spoke bitterly of the director who wanted to kick him out onto the street like a dog. I tried to reassure her: asking Rigola to suspend the run because Xavi was ill was like asking him to commit suicide.

'Besides, think of the other actors. They'd be affected, too.'

As I said all this, I took her tenderly by the hand. But neither my words nor my sympathetic gestures managed to soothe her.

From that point on, I increased the frequency of my visits. I would go three or four times a week, excluding Saturdays and Sundays. I didn't even bother to go home first. When I left work, I would take the number 22 bus and get off a few stops early to go by the supermarket. If there is anything I can say in my favour, it is that I always arrived with something to eat. Every evening, I offered to lay the table, change the baby or play with the little boy. It wasn't hard to get used to the house since, as I've said before, it always felt familiar to me. When I arrived, I would hang my coat on the rack and leave my briefcase in the hallway, then go straight to the kitchen to put away the things I had bought. Little by little I began turning into just another member of the family. I knew exactly where each plate went in the kitchen, knew how to set the table, even how to change the bed sheets if necessary. In the bathroom, where I liked to sit for ages, I would always find my two favourite magazines.

Just as he had declared he would, Xavi carried on working: as soon as he left the play, he started writing a novel. According to Josephina he was editing a manuscript that had been on the back burner for more than five years, a parody of the Spanish arts scene, particularly in Catalonia. It was humiliating watching him work. I'm sure his discipline and concentration would have made anyone feel bad, not just a sucker-fish like me. When it was time for dinner, Josephina would knock a few times at the door of the study to see if he wanted to join us or would rather eat at his desk. When he agreed to eat with us, he was always the one who brought a dose of cheer to the table. He would pick a record to put on, light a candle. The children would already be asleep by then, and the three of us would sit down without them to enjoy a nice hot soup. Unlike me, Xavi ate less and less as time went on. Sometimes he was so tired he struggled to hold his cutlery. Even so, he managed to finish the novel.

Shortly afterwards, Xavi Mestre went into Sant Pau hospital. Josephina was with him most of the time and, of course, the chores in the apartment multiplied. I tried to help her as much as I could, answering phone calls and, while I was at it, deleting from the answerphone Anna's messages dripping with emotional blackmail; she had by that point acquired the habit of insulting me. But I didn't have time for her fits of jealousy – I had to take care of bathing the children, making their dinner and putting them to bed. This was how I began staying there overnight. At first on the sofa, then with the children, who were always scared, and, when Josephina stayed over at the hospital, I would sleep in the marital bed, too.

Xavi died shortly before the end of winter. We held a funeral for him in Les Corts. It was a sad service, with more journalists than friends. I spent the whole morning there. My wife did not show up, and I thought better than to insist she did. In the afternoon, Josephina and I both ended up in the café at the funeral home. We sat down at one of the tables. It was nice in there. It was less cold, and the steamed-up windows obscured the view of the garden. I remember she was wearing a grey cashmere shawl. When I reached for her hand, I realized I no longer desired her. I'm certain that neither her pain nor the dramatic circumstances had anything to do with it. I asked her about the children, and she told me that her mother had taken them to Denmark that morning. She thanked me for having been so close by over the last few days.

'You showed Xavi that not all actors are as obnoxious as he thought.'

I merely smiled modestly.

When we said goodbye, Josephina announced that she was thinking about going back to Copenhagen and asked if I was interested in renting her apartment. I asked her to give me a few days to think about it.

THE ACCIDENTALS

Childhood does not end in one fell swoop, as we wished it would when we were children. It lingers, crouching silently in our adult, then wizened bodies, until one day, many years later, when we think that the heavy burden of bitterness and despair we've been shouldering has turned us irredeemably into adults, it reappears with the force and speed of a lightning bolt, wounding us with its freshness, its innocence, its unerring dose of naivety, but most of all with the certainty that this really and truly is the last glimpse we shall have of it. When we were children, precisely the opposite occurred: we dreamed of autonomy and the freedom to do whatever we wished, to use our time as we wanted, to choose what we ate, to move around as we pleased. Childhood felt like an interminable waiting room, a transitional stage between birth and the life we wanted to have. Children seldom realize their dreams: they lack the tools, depend on their parents, and neither Camilo's parents nor mine we particularly concerned with helping us to achieve ours. They were absorbed in and intoxicated by their own existence, trying to repair the disasters they were constantly leaving in their wake in their blundering dash towards who knows where. And so it was a stroke of luck to have a friend so close by. I would knock at Camilo's door and he could tell just by looking at me that my parents were having some kind of problem and that we had to find a safe haven for the rest of the afternoon, a place where no one could ask us to come back. Fortunately, there were many gardens in the surrounding area, dozens of shrubs we could hide behind.

The Palleiros arrived in Mexico in the mid-seventies, shortly after Camilo and I turned five. They were exiles from Uruguay, where the military junta had issued an arrest warrant for all Communists. They moved into the apartment block where I lived, but on the fourth floor, that is, right below my family's apartment. At that time many other exiled children came to live in the Villa Olímpica, sometimes accompanied by their parents, others by their aunts and uncles, or their grandparents. Not all families were able to emigrate at the same time, and not all of them got out intact. Those who had managed to pack up some things before moving had to wait months before they could go to the port where their belongings had been unloaded. The ones who had this privilege, though, were few and far between and so most of the time, their collection of household items was sparse, minimalist, modest: paper lampshades, items made of wicker or rustic wood, things gathered from here and there. Anything that might serve to construct this precarious nest.

There were more than twenty apartment blocks in the neighbourhood where we lived, and they were separated by tree-lined paths and stone slopes that were perfect for riding along on your bike. Every afternoon, when we got back from school, we children would scatter off down the paths in all directions, making the kind of racket you would hear during breaktime or at amusement parks. We shouted with different accents, from Mexico, Chile and Argentina, mainly. The Uruguayan accent was the least common and, perhaps for this reason, I thought it the prettiest. At dusk, the mothers would come out looking for us or wave from the windows for us to come home. We would all head inside, and then a silence as dark as night would settle over the gardens.

Camilo and I began playing together further back than I can remember. My first memories together with him date from when we were around six years old. I see us chasing a squirrel near the entrance to the car park, in endless fits of laughter. Two small children who live near each other making friends and playing together every day might sound predictable, but in our case it wasn't particularly. When they got to the city, his parents enrolled him in a school attended mainly by the children of workers affiliated with the Party, but he was too skinny, too tall, too clumsy and too cultured to escape notice (the best fate one can hope for in primary school). What's more, he wore glasses and spoke strangely. He would have been quite happy if his classmates had shown their dislike by ostracizing him instead of beating him up every day. But I was powerless to do anything about his predicament, just as he couldn't prevent the fact that at my school, a private Montessori one, I was bullied due to my extreme shyness. We shared the fortune, both good and bad, of being the children of absent, lefty parents. And we shared, too, the urgent need to grow up, to build our own lives, which we imagined free from the stresses and strains of family. Two futures very different to each other; for while I dreamed of piloting planes, scaling mountains and travelling via airship, he spoke only of returning to Uruguay. I wonder where this obsession can have come from, since as far as I can recall, at his house, where I spent as much time as he did at mine, the idea was never spoken of.

The gardens, like the apartment blocks, had their own tenants. Whole families of snails, birds and stray cats inhabited the hedges and the branches of the trees. The birds were by far my favourites. I wasn't interested in hunting them with a catapult like the other children did, but rather in sitting down to watch them. I liked the fact that their songs, their colours, their size and their plumage were all so different, and that some were free, and others lived in cages inside people's apartments, like the children whose parents never let them come down to the local square to mingle with everyone else. It is true that most of the birds around us were 'gross pigeons', as Camilo called them, but there were also sparrows and American robins with their orange beaks. The birds in people's homes were predominantly canaries, finches and domestic parrots. Whenever I was ill and lucky enough to miss school, I would listen to the birds from my bedroom, amazed at the din they made which, in the afternoons, we would drown out with our shouts.

My father quickly developed an interest in birds and for many years this constituted one of the subjects we were always able to talk about. We invented a game that consisted of observing our neighbours and figuring out which kind of bird they most resembled, whether due to their physical appearance or their behaviour. The lady on the ground floor, Lalo's mother, was clearly an owl with five fledglings in the nest; the woman in number 305, a stiletto-wearing robin. Camilo picked up the game right away and became even better than I was at identifying the birds concealed behind people.

Ernesto Palleiro, Camilo's father – a flamingo, not only because of the intense hue of his ideology – liked playing guitar, drinking wine and smoking unfiltered cigarettes. We would listen to him from his son's bedroom, just as we listened to my parents' fights, barely muffled by the walls and ceiling. The sounds travelled in the opposite direction, too. Frequently I would be woken in the middle of the night by Camilo's crying, cries I would have recognized from miles away, and on hearing them, I'd be filled with an overwhelming rage towards his parents for not taking him out of that damned school where he was being tortured. As I drifted back to sleep, I would tell myself that he likely wasn't the only one to feel that way, and that in each one of these buildings of exiles, there was at least one child crying themselves to sleep every night.

Shortly before my eleventh birthday, my father finished his doctorate in biology and was offered a research position at the University of New Orleans. This was how, one day out of the blue, after having lived always in the same habitat, we too packed up our things and migrated north. Camilo and I said goodbye to each other at the entrance to our building, making promises about the future, but knowing deep down that it was highly unlikely we would ever see each other again.

That moment ushered in a period of instability for my family, and was the start of a series of peregrinations which took us to different American and European cities. My father accepted work where he was offered it, almost always at prestigious universities, but for quite short periods of time. My mother and I followed him. In all these cities my parents argued with an identical fervour. Their clashes were the only constant in the various houses we lived in, and I am inclined to think that in these dramatic quarrels they found some sort of equilibrium: the more they argued, the more united they seemed.

In New Orleans, the sea was close by. There were seagulls instead of pigeons. When he had time, Dad would take me to look at birds, birds that lived free in the forest or in the state's bayous. One weekend we visited the reserve at Cat Island in the southeast of Louisiana, which has a rookery of brown pelicans. We travelled first by car and then in a boat belonging to the university, with a team of biologists – one of them a friend of my father's – and a couple of sailors. The atmosphere on board was festive and relaxed. The sailors made fun of the biologists, and the biologists told jokes about sailors. My father's friend took out a fishing rod. Very soon he got a bite from a long, pinkish-coloured fish, which he put in a bucket. The idea was to catch enough for all of us and then roast them once we got back to land. After the third or fourth one, the rod began to bend, and we had to hold onto its owner so the weight didn't pull him into the water. At first we thought it was a really big fish, but then, as we dragged the creature on board, we discovered in utter horror that the animal pulling on the hook was a gigantic bird.

'Let go of the rod!' shouted one of the sailors. 'It's got its beak hooked!'

I asked my father if it was a pelican, but he put me right: the creature beating its two immense, clumsy wings against the deck of the boat was an albatross.

The sailors stared in astonishment at the injured bird, while one of the biologists tried to open its beak to take out the hook. It wasn't easy – the bird was writhing around with a furious flapping of its wings, trying to escape. Its squawks revealed the rage and fear it was feeling. What was an albatross doing so far away from its natural habitat? My father's friend explained that it was very rare to see them outside of their geographical range, but that from time to time it happens that one is pulled off course by a storm and gets lost. The problem, he said, isn't that they go beyond their territory, but rather than when they do, it's very hard for them to cross the equator and return to it. Eventually the biologist managed to get the bit of metal out and, after several wobbly attempts to walk across the deck, the albatross flapped its wings to take off. Once in the air, it spread its wings and hovered majestically over the boat, allowing us to gaze at it for a few more minutes. Someone started clapping, and we all joined in.

When I got home, I wrote to Camilo to tell him that at last I knew which bird he was, but thought better of it before finishing the letter.

Towards the end of secondary school, my family emigrated to the south of France, and I started attending the Lycée Mignet d'Avignon. My classmates were going through a seemingly endless rutting season. Engrossed in their various mating dances, they would do anything they could to get a romantic partner, but then later, halfway through the year, they would swap one mate for another, and then another. It was around this time that I wrote the first letter, a letter three pages long with small, cramped handwriting in which I told Camilo about the main events of recent times, including the discovery of the albatross on Cat Island, but also the loneliness I felt. Books were my only stable friendships during those years. I would get home and read until overcome by sleep. I thought often of Camilo. I wondered what he was like now, physically. I myself had changed a lot: I was taller, more gangly, and my nose seemed as if it would never stop growing. I wondered if his face was covered in spots as had happened to so many of the boys at my school, if his voice was the same or had transformed into an unrecognizable squawk, but none of these questions remained in the letter. I posted it not knowing if he would receive it. After all, four years had gone by, and it was highly likely his parents had moved. A month later I received a photo of his new skateboard, on which he had painted a pair of large, two-tone wings. On the back he had written: 'Love, Camilo.'

It was that same year, in my French literature class that they made me read *Les fleurs du mal*, and I went to request it from the school library. No sooner had they handed me the book than I opened a page at random and the poem about the albatross appeared before me: '*ces rois de l'azur, maladroits et honteux*,' where Baudelaire posits it as the *poète maudit* of nature. I read it to my father that same night. He, in turn, and very eagerly, read to me the poem in which Coleridge tells the story of a sailor who is damned forever for killing an albatross. The text, as dark as any I've read, troubled me immensely. *All men of the sea know this story*, my father said. I understood, then, the horror of the sailor in Louisiana when he'd seen that his fishing rod had got caught in the beak of that great bird. I copied out a verse by hand to send it to Camilo in answer to his photograph. I hadn't had a boyfriend in that whole period. I like to get to know people well before even thinking about giving them a kiss, and the boys would become exasperated. I was too clumsy, too slow.

In December 1983 the dictatorship ended in Argentina and Raúl Alfonsín came to power. Half of the inhabitants of Villa Olímpica went back home. I found this out from the neighbours who had been in touch with my parents this whole time and were now trying to sell their cars or their apartments. Democracy returned to Uruguay in 1985. We were still away from Mexico. I asked my father to write to the Palleiros to find out what their plans were and, before they could reply, I received a disconsolate letter from Camilo, in which he disparaged his family for refusing to return.

A few years later we took a trip to Patagonia. My father wanted to see the glaciers and I the albatrosses, this time in their natural habitat. We visited the Islas Malvinas, a place known for having an immense colony of black-browed albatrosses. We found the islands covered in adolescent birds who had just returned to their place of origin. They had been born there four or five years earlier and, as soon as they had been reared, had spent that same amount of time flying across the ocean, scarcely touching land. But instinct, that force comparable only to fate, compels the albatross to return and establish themselves not just in their country, but merely a few feet from where they were born, too. On this island we found a nest with an abandoned egg. It was explained to us that this was an unusual tragedy: if an albatross abandons its home, it can only be in order to save its life. When I heard this story, I thought about my South American neighbours, who returned home as soon as it was possible to the country where they had been on the point of death. It wasn't easy. There were few jobs, and people were suspicious of them; they looked at them as one watches the disappeared return.

I have vivid and conflicting memories of that trip to Patagonia. In my imagination the albatross was quite a rare and solitary bird, and seeing them living together in their colonies seemed almost an oxymoron. But the world – I know from experience – is full of strange birds that do not even suspect this is what they are. As if this weren't enough, all those albatrosses were focused on a single thing: mating. And their attitude was just as perplexing as that of my contemporaries in nightclubs or the playground. The albatross's courtship phase is perhaps the longest in all the animal kingdom. They can spend two years or more dancing around other individuals, until they find the one with whom they can synchronize their movements. Except that, unlike my classmates at the lycée, the albatross is monogamous, and long-lived. For them, it is normal to take care when choosing a partner.

A year after this trip, my father died. He was found in a hotel room in Mexico City, having suffered a heart attack. My mother and I went back to hold the wake and to arrange laying him to rest in a cemetery which overlooks the Valle de Bravo lake, to the west of Mexico City. We received many phone calls during those days. My mother took them all, even those from my friends, as I was in no state to speak to anyone. One evening, she mentioned that Camilo had rung.

If you think about it, the custom of visiting the places where our beloveds' bones are is absurd, but in that errant life of ours, my family was my only nest, my only burrow. This is why I visit my father's grave whenever I go to Mexico and when I do, I try to bring a bit of honey with me to attract the hummingbirds. My father would often say that people only gain recognition in Mexico when they make a career for themselves abroad. I don't know if he was right, but it was certainly true in his case. A year after his death, the Faculty of Science organized a symposium in his memory, and invited me and my mother to open it. The main lecture theatre was packed full of academics of all generations, and this was where I encountered him once again, in the middle of the crowd. Although he had changed enormously, it didn't take me more than a second or two to recognize him. We hugged each other without a word, in front of all those professors who were so renowned, so earnest. We arranged to meet the following day, in a café in Coyoacán. We spent the whole afternoon recounting our lives to one another. I talked to him about the cities I'd lived in, and I talked, too, about the albatross. He explained he still lived in Villa Olímpica, in the same apartment, putting up with the cooing of the dirty, monotonous pigeons. He told me he had had a car accident: a friend had tried to beat a train to a level crossing and had lost. Because of him, Camilo had spent three months in hospital, fighting for the use of his leg. The experience had given him the push he'd needed to finish his economics degree, but he didn't work in anything related, as he lacked the patience. He helped his father with his screen-printing business and in exchange, his father, divorced a few years back, fed and housed him. Ernesto Palleiro didn't suspect a thing about the marijuana being grown under artificial light by Camilo in the wardrobe in his bedroom, so he could then sell it to the neighbours. His father's strict Communist values would have prevented him from forgiving his son. Villa Olímpica has historically been a neighbourhood where cannabis is consumed. He was in the perfect place. He assured me that he was saving everything he earned to return one day to Uruguay. Despite his insistence, I turned down his invitation to go and visit them. I still felt quite fragile after my father's death, and the mere idea of setting foot in my old neighbourhood again terrified me. There would be time for that. We met another couple of times in the same café, and each time we stayed there until they kicked us out. When we left, we would walk round and round the block. We couldn't stop talking or staring at each other. We took note of the physical changes with admiration and surprise: his hair, which before had been poker straight, had grown curly, and he no longer wore glasses. But he was still just as tall, and his hugs just as perfect.

Without saying a word to him, I missed my flight back to France to stay by his side and since then I haven't taken up my studies again. You can quantify the effects of tangible accidents, but internal blows leave imperceptible scars that are much harder to mend. I rented an apartment close to the university, and it was there that we would meet up a couple of times a week. My contribution was the space itself with its terrace. His was the pizza, along with the wine and the weed. Those get-togethers consisted of us telling each other the details of our lives, and of laughing at each other until we cried. Sometimes Camilo would miss our meeting or cancel it at the last minute to go out with other, potentially compatible female friends. He had lots, but none of them lasted. I liked the fact that he told me about his failures, as if he knew that with me there was no need to keep up appearances or our distance. And I really didn't judge him, just as he didn't judge my decision to wait however many years it took before pair-bonding with someone.

We spent almost six months like this, synchronized, with a harmony akin to that of our childhood, until the time I finally accepted his invitation to go and visit him in Villa Olímpica. His father had gone out of town, and we set ourselves up in his house from noon on Friday. On the Saturday afternoon, we went out for a walk. Camilo could recall perfectly the places where we used to play or go and hide. 'You used to like taking your dolls here, and this is where we buried our stash of sweets, and this is where the water balloon fight that lasted three days started, behind these bushes.' I asked him about Paula, Facundo and all the other neighbours who came to my mind that day. Camilo told me about their lives up until the moment they left Mexico. He had seen all of them leave, one after another. 'I didn't hear anything from them once they'd left. I'm the only one who's still here. And my folks, of course, but those idiots are just too frightened.' We were walking together along the stony paths, hand in hand, but in reality we were on two opposite tracks: I was going back to childhood, whereas he wanted only to flee from it.

That night, we smoked more than usual and ended up in his room. The bed seemed as wide as a clear night sky in which we pursued each other, slipping with our wings wide open along dizzying currents of tropical air. I awoke with a headache and the feeling of having done a parachute jump. Camilo's clothes were on the floor, all mixed up with my own.

On the Monday, I went back home and didn't hear from him the whole week. I respected his silence. He called on the Thursday night to tell me he had bought his ticket and was going to leave for Montevideo in a week. I received the news without a word. *You don't need to pretend*, he said. *I know you're crying*. I laughed and told him between sobs that he was a prick. That is all I said. I didn't ask him to stay; how could I if it was all he had ever wanted, if in his life nothing memorable had happened except for his two accidents, which in my opinion were nothing but failed attempts at escaping captivity? It was a debt he had with his history and his family, even if they refused to acknowledge it. I would also have liked to ask him which was really his country: Mexico, where he had been living for two decades, or Uruguay, of which he didn't even have one miserable memory? But of all the things I might have said to him that night, there was nothing he wouldn't already have thought of a thousand times. My interrogation wouldn't have contributed much to his inner dialogue. My only job now was to accompany him as he got ready for the journey, help him to pack his things, drive him to the storage facility he'd rented to leave them there, and then finally take him to the airport, trying to prevent poor Ernesto Palleiro, sitting in the back of the car, mute as a man on his way to a funeral, from seeing me cry.

That afternoon, Camilo's father and I stood next to each other in the airport's viewing gallery for a couple of hours, until the LATAM plane crossed the sky with its two-tone wings. In the car on the way back home, I told him about the albatross I had seen as a girl. These birds, I explained, have a very clearly defined territory: the North Pacific and the southern hemisphere, to be precise. However, there are times when sailors come across one of these birds in highly unusual places, as happened to me and my father on the islands of Louisiana. They call them 'vagrant albatrosses', or sometimes 'accidentals'. Of all the birds in the world, I told Ernesto, the albatrosses are the best flyers. They simply have to spread their immense wings and they soar, following the fluctuations of the wind. But it's true, too, that without wind they cannot get anywhere. Sometimes when they try to, they go mad, die of exhaustion, and fall into the ocean. They may also land on a boat and accompany it, or establish themselves in places completely different from their natural habitat. When they are lost, they pair up without ceremony, with females of hugely disparate species of albatross which, like them, have become vagrants. Ever since I found out they existed, I told him, I have wondered what leads them to form these kinds of unions, these birds who are usually so scrupulous about choosing a partner. Is it the need to pair up with anyone at all? Camilo's father was silent. Or perhaps it's the opposite, I went on: a bird with an experience as powerful as that of being lost and not being able to fly home can only mate with a female who is just as lost. In the unlikely case that one of them wants – and is able – to return, does it cease to be an accidental? And then, once again, I asked Ernesto Palleiro, who by now was looking at me warily, like someone who has before them a person who is losing their mind: after twenty years of putting down roots in another country, can you integrate back into your original colony just like that?

'I don't know,' he replied eventually. And didn't open his mouth again for the rest of the journey.

THE TORPOR

Five hours have gone by since my husband and the children went to sleep. The sky was still light when the three of them got into their respective beds wearing their masks. They sleep with the fan on because otherwise the heat keeps them awake. Initially, I would go to bed early, too. I adopted a daytime rhythm when my husband did. Now we have dinner shortly before seven and, by nine, we're all in bed. The children don't even protest. On the contrary, they find it thrilling. At night we can finally detach ourselves, stop seeing each other's faces and make a separate life. In dreams I am not married, or not always, and nor do I have a family; I swim in the sea, climb mountains and see my friends again, as well as people I've had no news of in a long time. At first the rest did me good, but then I realized that, with every day that passes, I want to sleep more, greedily, not because I need to but because dreams are the most interesting thing going on in my life. After a while, none of us wanted to get up at seven any more. Sleeping so many hours worries me. I've told them a thousand times, but they ignore me. I have to really persevere if I want to wake them up early, and when I manage it, they complain that I'm interrupting them. I like the ritual of breakfast, of starting the day together and telling each other about all the exciting dreams we've had, before turning to our screens to focus on work, but it bores them.

It's been over fifteen years since the world changed completely and we passed into 'locked-down mode', this intramural life we've been leading ever since the virus appeared. The university where I work closed its classrooms in the first year and adopted distance learning. At first no one imagined this would become the norm;

everyone kept a close eye on the curve of infections and deaths. They made predictions about when all this would end. However, when most countries implemented a universal basic income, young people no longer had a reason to go to university, and many of my fellow lecturers lost their jobs. My case is a little different: literature is one of the few degrees that hasn't been damaged by the lockdown. People have more time to read now, and there are some who like to do so methodically. I have never seen my students, except on the screen, and this helps to avoid any of the extra-professional attachments such as we used to see. The scandals due to affairs between students and their teachers ended; the marks we give are more objective. The department of literature I'm attached to is divided into two areas of research: pre- and post-pandemic literature. In my opinion, the most brilliant youngsters are among those who are interested in the world just as it was before, even if, for some of them, finding out how we used to live can turn out to be quite disturbing. Our loss has been colossal, and discovering this can send you mad.

Education is not only obligatory for children, it now comes with huge penalties if they do not comply. Their families may be deprived of the not inconsiderable family allowance. In a sense, the children are the ones who maintain their parents. At the end of term, those who perform better at school receive a holiday premium, which allows them to purchase video games and more time on recreational platforms. It has to be said that the incentive works and is not as disinterested as it might appear. When they finish secondary education, the government selects the best students and compels them to study on pre-assigned degree programmes. Some are chosen to be doctors, others physicists, still others electricians. There is no way for those selected to choose their own profession, and nor are they able to resign from it. The ones who end up in my virtual classroom are very different. What is most likely is that they've never made any effort to be in the dominant group, and purely for this reason I have an especially soft spot for them.

The young people who ended up halfway between today's education and the previous one are called 'the lost generation'. It is suspected that the basic income is a temporary measure and serves only to stop those kids from going out into the streets and stealing or organizing protests as we did, over ten years ago, when we came out of lockdown for the first time. Infection rates in the city had gone down a lot, and for a couple of months, the bars opened up again. Cinemas and theatres went back to putting things on. In the Bois de Vincennes, people started organizing spontaneous parties; they would spring up suddenly, without anyone having seen them coming. Someone would play a guitar, someone else would bring a set of speakers. People took turns putting music on. We all danced. There was an urgent feeling, as if this might be the last chance we had to be together. A few of us also started to demonstrate. The pandemic had opened our eyes, and we were demanding from our politicians more equality, and more respect for the environment, too. I was twenty-three years old and had an uncontainable rage. I blamed our rulers for having stolen my future. They had failed to manage any of the crises around us. We hated them, and dreamed of only one thing: to do away with them, to escape from their ever tighter grip. My generation made the malaise of the Earth their own.

It was on one of these marches that I met Benoît. A couple of years older than me, he studied history at the same university where I had begun studying literature. On the weekends he would help farmers sell their produce in the market held every Sunday on the Boulevard Richard-Lenoir. I have always believed it was love at first sight, that recognition that Novalis and André Breton spoke of, but it's also true that we didn't have a lot of time. As almost always happened, the police blocked our path and began trying to constrain us. We had to disperse, not without first throwing bottles or any blunt object we had to hand at them. In the chaos I lost one of my shoes, and Benoît lent me his so that I could run without hurting myself. That night I slept at his house. In the morning, he walked me home and, although he was a total stranger to them, began explaining to my parents why we were getting home at that time. I think this made them warm to him. Older people were carrying a huge sense of guilt towards us, and it was easy for them to forgive us anything. Benoît and I continued to see each other every day. But this period was brief: before long, infections multiplied, and we were locked down once again, this time more strictly. Those months of freedom, this breath of air, was dubbed 'the recess' by historians, and they maintain that its consequences were so disastrous and long-lasting that it will be studied indefinitely. Over the following months, more people than ever died. The images shown on the television with bodies stacked up in mass graves were unbearable. Benoît lost his two best friends. People were frightened and felt responsible. This is why they accepted without hesitation the government's orders. Since we didn't live together, Benoît and I were obliged to stop seeing each other. We would speak on the phone at all hours, yearning desperately for physical contact. We had to come up with strategies to meet as soon as possible, and they all involved defying the police.

After that second period of lockdown, the state took control of the press, arguing that reporters were highly active agents of infection, leading everyone to fear them, even more than doctors. Propagating this irrational fear towards journalists was one of their best control tactics. Now, in order to keep informed, we can only rely on rumours. We know how crucial it is that they be reliable, and this is why it is so frowned upon to spread them around without first making sure that the information they contain is correct. The official news, what you see on TV and in printed papers – which have preserved their names but in no way the spirit that inspired them when they were first established – claims that society is peaceful, that infections are finally starting to come down, except in poorer neighbourhoods and countries, which they show endless images of, claiming that this is why it is of the utmost importance to remain isolated. They do not mention the temperature, or the floods in Scandinavia which, it is said, have caused a huge number of deaths. The news bulletins stopped covering climate change as a political topic a long time ago, and turned it instead into an urban legend, a superstition held by uninformed people.

In the gloom of their bedroom, my children sleep blithely on, surrendered to those dreamscapes they protect so fiercely. I imagine them flying around in paragliders, soaring over mountains and lakes, free as birds with enormous wings, or on a pair of skis, the cold mountain air rushing over their faces. Despite the fact that we're now in November, the heat is still unbearable. I have old memories of a time when it still snowed in winter. My siblings and I would go out into the park to play. We have all started to doubt these memories. My friend Charlotte claims that they are hangovers from the dreams we have every night, and that prolonging one's hours of rest produces this kind of reaction, a sort of false or invented memory. Now, the only thing we are aware of from the outside world are ambulance sirens and the sound of the trucks that every day bring food and gas to our homes. There is also the news in the papers and on social media, but we do not know whether to believe it or not. There are those who claim that news reports are produced by artificial intelligence, just like the images of people who have been hospitalized or the long queues waiting for medical attention outside local clinics. I can't deny that we have got used to it. No one is waiting for the end of lockdown any longer. We have reinvented the world, created a new normal, as people called it in the beginning, and we have adapted to it. This is what's worst of all.

There were also, of course, those who never obeyed the government's restrictive measures or those who, once the first year had gone by, opted to rebel against the system and to live in a less controlled manner. Whole groups of people escaped to the countryside, and in the very depths of the forest, set up clandestine communities. Via the farmers he used to work with, Benoît came into contact with one of these groups, a self-sufficient community which grew and produced its own food. Among them were architects, physicists, farmers, craftsmen, doctors. We had an interview with two of them via video call. We explained that we didn't know how to do anything except tell stories, but this too was welcomed. Everything else we would learn along the way. I was the one who insisted we join them, and Benoît agreed. As soon as the move was formalized, we were sent nurses' uniforms and papers from the Hôpital Saint-Louis which meant we could move around outside without calling attention to ourselves. Dressed in our disguises, Benoît and I were met one afternoon at the edge of Vincennes by a lad in an ambulance, who drove us deep into the forest.

The commune was very well hidden, and if it was difficult to access, it was even harder to leave without a guide. Although there were lots of people moving from one spot to another, fetching and carrying boxes of medicine and food, it wasn't a joyful place as I had imagined: some people had lost their families and lamented their loss with heart-wrenching sobs. No sooner had we arrived than they confiscated our medical uniforms as well as our phones. No one was allowed to use them if we wanted to stay hidden. We began working that same afternoon, chopping up old bits of furniture to turn into firewood. In the evening, we washed and peeled potatoes in the kitchen. It wasn't long before I began to miss my parents. I had lived with them until that point, and I dreamed of leaving to go and get them and bring them back with us. Benoît said it was far too soon, that first we should figure out if we'd be able to adapt to this new regime. He was right. Life in the community was anything but easy. We slept in shared spaces where intimacy was simply impossible. There weren't many couples who slept together in front of everyone else, but the overcrowding not only stopped me from feeling like having sex at night, it also kept me awake. As well as the physical work, which was gruelling, you had to deal with a range of very different people, some generous and supportive who cared for the elderly, others selfish, who stole food supplies from the store houses. Benoît and I were suspicious of everyone. Whenever I had a free moment, I would slip away from the group and head deeper into the forest, regardless of the time of day or night. Walking in nature restored to me the dignity that the government had snatched away. It was so lovely to listen to the birds, hear them flying or fluttering around in the scrub. One morning I found myself face to face with a family of foxes drinking water from a stream. A mother with three cubs. I squatted down behind some bushes so as not to frighten them, but even so, she immediately sensed my presence. Instead of running off as I had feared, she held my gaze for several seconds. Her acorn-coloured eyes seemed to contain immeasurable sweetness, as if she felt sorry for me. Not long after, I heard the steps of her companions on the grass. A pack of foxes of varying sizes was trotting quickly through the forest. It was like a sudden burst of life, a lesson in freedom. The family went to join them, and they all disappeared into the trees. When I told him, Benoît started to come with me on my walks and it was there, almost in the same place I had seen the foxes, that we conceived our first child.

What can have become of our commune and all the others? Rumour has it that the police have dismantled quite a few of them and their inhabitants are serving sentences in insalubrious prisons where they almost immediately contract the virus and die. Hardly any countries in the world employ the death penalty any more. Liberty always has a price, which is why there are so many different, personal forms of dissidence. For instance, there are the mystics who, instead of sleeping like we do, meditate, pray or practise visualizations. They claim, so as to convince us to follow in their footsteps, that during the years of lockdown many people have obtained enlightenment. They refer to themselves as 'practitioners' and speak of an invisible, asymptomatic happiness whenever they are interviewed on the television. There are people who claim these groups are fictitious, but I know this isn't true. Some of my friends without children opted for that path. When you do have kids, you simply cannot permit yourself this. What kind of existence would a child abandoned in an apartment have while Mummy and Daddy sit and meditate endlessly in their room?

When he found out he was going to be a father, Benoît was gripped with fear. While before he'd had his doubts with regards to the commune, now he began to view as unsustainable this existence that I felt made sense despite its limitations and the great physical work it demanded. Staying there, he said, would be like building a house on the edge of a precipice. We might be found at any moment. Bringing children into the world in such uncertain conditions was to condemn them before birth. For him it was about two ways of life that were simply irreconcilable. It was possible to have an abortion in the commune – a few of our female friends had already done so and, although it wasn't obligatory, the leaders recommended it. For me, though, this wasn't an option: I wanted more than anything to have this child. For Benoît, it was a choice between staying there without any offspring or starting a family.

With the same efficiency he had orchestrated our escape, Benoît organized our return. Not only did he arrange for us to be transported by car, he also got hold of a marriage certificate from the *mairie* in Fontainebleau, which allowed us to live together in society. We weren't able to say goodbye to our fellow commune dwellers: what we were doing was considered treason. Twice now we had been dissidents. But the laws of our country take in without objection those who repent, and we exercised these rights so we could return.

We had no problem finding a house. Many have been built since the start of the pandemic, social housing blocks with big windows that look out onto walls covered in ivy, or little internal courtyards. The aim was to prevent people from living on the streets, and to ensure that the greatest possible number of residents would produce and consume everything from home. Of course, there are still a few pariahs. More than ever, society is polarized between those who live in absolute comfort, but without leaving our homes, and those who, every day, die exposed to the elements.

Since we returned to the city, I haven't seen my parents again. Family visits are prohibited. Any contact we have with them and with my parents-in-law has been on video calls. We arrange to speak once a week and to celebrate our birthdays. They are always surprised by how much the children have grown. I suppose they say this because of their faces, since they've never seen them standing up, or their whole bodies. If it's difficult for us, it must be far more so for them. My husband has taken the precaution of recording hours and hours of these conversations. He says that, thanks to this, when our parents die, the children won't miss them. They will still be there on the screen, as they have always seen them. Now, my husband assures me, we have a record of their voices and hundreds of facial expressions that we can edit to make them say new things, to hand out advice or congratulations whenever necessary. It will be as if they'd never left, he exclaims enthusiastically. Meanwhile, I am consoled by the thought of not having left too many photos or videos of myself, except from my classes at the university.

The heat is easier to bear when you're asleep. When I see my husband lying on our bed, I want to lie down, too, to lose myself in some dreamy adventure, but I know that if I do this I will stay there for the rest of the night, and I don't want to sleep more than is necessary. Six hours at the most, preferably four. Discretely, so Benoît doesn't notice, I drag the bedroom fan over to the desk where I'm writing. I'm not wearing clothes either, just knickers and a vest. By my side sits a thermos of cold water, which I take regular gulps from. It's been a week since the supply truck came by, and our refrigerator is still overflowing with fruit and vegetables. This confirms my fears: by sleeping so much we are eating less. I don't like waste, I say this frequently to my two children, while Benoît makes a face at me, but my words ricochet off the walls of his absent ears. For years we would make an effort to have fun and play games as a family. It was enough to be healthy and all together. My husband and the children gave me all the love I might need. We touched each other, kissed each other, sniffed each other, bit each other's ears. Benoît would say that doing this produced endorphins, the happiness hormones, but the day came when we grew tired of this, too. The sarcastic comments and reproachful glances have become more and more frequent.

It is almost three o'clock in the morning. I really ought to prepare my class now if I want to get up with my family at nine, make breakfast, and be ready by eleven. My students, just like my husband and my children, will wear on their faces the blissful smile of someone who has slept well. I will offer them the bags under my eyes and the wrinkles that, as I confirm in front of the mirror each morning, are growing more and more pronounced. I don't regret it; it's the price I pay for what I believe in. Life leaves its mark upon those who dare to look at it head on, lucidly.

Some mornings I wake up suffocating, on the verge of a panic attack, wishing I could run for hours. In those moments, my refuge is the balcony in the kitchen from where you can see a small slice of sky. I tell myself that this five-metre square space is the only thing that distinguishes this house from a mausoleum. Meanwhile, my husband sinks down further into sleep as if he were wearing a diving suit. Sleeping: I think that in the end, this became his most personal form of dissidence. For my part, I have begun dreaming of going back to the forest. Not to the commune, but deeper in, where only the animals live and, if I'm lucky, perhaps, to find that pack of foxes again. Benoît is probably right when he says I wouldn't even last a week there. That might be the case, but at least it would be a beautiful week, a real week, full of smells and of sounds. I would have to go alone; this is something I have already accepted. It's just a question of deciding. If I do it, what will become of my family? Probably they will forget me as they forget everything, and eventually grow used to my absence. Perhaps they will even end up believing that they knew me only from a dream.

The authorized representative in the EEA is
eucomply OÜ, Pärnu mnt 139b-14, 11317 Tallinn, Estonia.
hello@eucompliancepartner.com
+33757690241

This book is printed with plant-based inks on materials
certified by the Forest Stewardship Council®. The FSC®
promotes an ecologically, socially and economically
responsible management of the world's forests. This book
has been printed without the use of plastic-based coatings.

Fitzcarraldo Editions
8-12 Creekside
London, SE8 3DX
Great Britain

Copyright © Guadalupe Nettel, 2023
c/o Indent Literary Agency
First published in 2023 as *Los divagantes*
Translation copyright © Rosalind Harvey, 2025
This first edition published in Great Britain
by Fitzcarraldo Editions in 2025

The right of Guadalupe Nettel to be identified as the
author of this work has been asserted in accordance with
Section 77 of the Copyright, Designs and Patents Act 1988.

ISBN 978-1-80427-147-6

Design by Ray O'Meara
Typeset in Fitzcarraldo
Printed and bound by Pureprint

All rights reserved. No part of this publication may be
reproduced, stored in a retrieval system or transmitted
in any form or by any means, electronic, mechanical,
photocopying, recording or otherwise, without prior
permission in writing from Fitzcarraldo Editions.

fitzcarraldoeditions.com

Fitzcarraldo Editions